H

After twenty years' mindless toil in graphic design ('I worked on the My Little Pony account') Tim Earnshaw neatly sidestepped an impending mid-life crisis by moving to France, where he fulfilled a lifetime's ambition ('mine, not hers') to live off his wife in a foreign country.

In between 'cleaning' the apartment and burning the shopping, he has found time to pen this, his first novel. *Helium* is set in California because the author has never been there. 'But,' he says, 'I watch a lot of *Charlie's Angels* re-runs dubbed into French.'

Tim Earnshaw became a writer because he has no mates.

TIM EARNSHAW

Helium

VICTOR GOLLANCZ

LONDON

First published in Great Britain 1997
by Victor Gollancz
An imprint of the Cassell Group
Wellington House, 125 Strand, London WC2R 0BB

A Gollancz Paperback Original

Copyright © Tim Earnshaw 1997

The right of Tim Earnshaw to be identified as author of
this work has been asserted by him in accordance with
the Copyright, Designs and Patents Act, 1988.

A catalogue record for this book is
available from the British Library.

ISBN 0 575 06471 4

Typeset by CentraCet, Cambridge
Printed by Guernsey Press Co Ltd,
Guernsey, Channel Isles

97 98 99   5 4 3 2 1

This is dedicated to the one I love

LISSA

Strange how such a solitary occupation relies
on so much selfless support:

Everything: Claire Couldwell

I'll wear it always: Simon Nye

Mystery Switch: Jonny Geller

Guitar, vocal: Mike Petty

Plugs and points: Katrina Whone

Bunting: Gillian Holmes

Claudia Stumpfl: Claudia Stumpfl

Central marginalia: Claire Calman

Tazer enthusiasm: Joanna Isles

Kirlian Aura combing: Anthea Kemp, Pierre Vivant

Lucozade: John Gillett, Sara Roberts

Lumbar support: Sir James Tanburn

He's American: Peter Fisher

Salami: Alexander McGillivray

Laundry: Clive Hetherington

ONE

Something Weird

—Want to see something weird?

Gary squeegeed the bathroom mirror with the ledge of his hand. His hair was floating.

—Stunt hair. Static, I guess. Real poetic. Like an underwater fern.

He looked in the cabinet for some greasy kid stuff to stick it down, found a tub of blue gel Marcie had bought him, what, five, six years back. Jesus. And his fucking disciples. He sank his fingers into the clammy goo and wiped it on his hair, lowering his gaze to the pale, hairy bulb of his belly. Monday mornings were traditionally set aside for a starkly pitiless appraisal; Gary Wilder: The Wilderness Years – Failure and Waste in Modern America.

—Forty-five years down the fucking toilet.

He cursed the government, the economy and his ex-wife.

—Even took the shower curtain. What kind of woman takes the fucking shower curtain for fuck's sake.

He ran a comb through his hair, laying it in a shiny slick back from his forehead, thinking the whole Marcie thing over again, using the familiar litany of hindsight.

—Never told me exactly why she left, never gave me that consideration, nope, never showed me the courtesy of a discussion, just looked me up and down in that heavy-lidded way she had and said, go figure. Look at the fucking water all over the shop, I mean it's a fucking aquarium for fuck's sake.

He curled his lip and snarled at his hair.

—You look like a wetback pimp son of a bitch sportscaster.

He padded back to the perma-gloom of his bedroom and pulled on a stale Barry Manilow tour sweat. In the kitchen he squinted at the sunlight bouncing off the smeary worksurfaces like it was trying to give him a headache. His dad had fitted out the kitchen back in the early seventies with pale turquoise units he'd salvaged from somewhere, and they'd never fit the square plan here. Big grief from his mom day one. Okay, his dad said, very quietly, you do kitchens from now on. And the house, a white cinderblock bungalow with green Spanish tiled roof, had stayed unchanged since then. Gary didn't do kitchens either.

—Already too hot to think about tapdancing as a career option, he said to himself. Could shut up early and mellow out at the coast before visiting the old guy, or leave Carl to mind the store all day and just head into the hills with some beers and get headachey. Maybe borrow Big Dave's Colt and shoot some fucking trees or flowers.

He rinsed a mug in the sink and stared absently at Gretchen hanging out the wash in Vandergelder's yard. The yards here were all the same, big squares of bleached crabgrass bordered by nameless straggling shrubbery, rubbed bare round bent basketball hoops with no nets. Cracked patios, broken barbecues. Light a barbecue now, some punk gets a bead on your ass with a crossbow. Gary guessed Gretchen was about twenty, twenty-five. Hard to say. Her brown-blond hair just touching her shoulders and her bare arms as she reached up, and green pegs in her mouth like dinosaur teeth. She saw him and waved a big pair of gray jockeys. He waved the dishcloth back.

—God knows I have done my best to entertain wild sexual fantasies about that girl. Low carnality quotient, name like Gretchen. Like Heidi, a bit Nazi. Nice kid, though. Yeah, yoo-hoo.

He felt his hair stiffening against his scalp, and slid his fingers over the flat blades, reminding him of the bones of a sea-ray he'd eaten out at the point. He heard Vandergelder's reedy voice calling for Gretchen. She made a face and disappeared. She was the live-in help, and some kind of relation, but of course people talked. Vandergelder was soaking up a disability pension, and liked her to push him up and down the mall in his wheelchair and a plaid rug so people could see how sick he was. One night Gary had caught him creeping about setting rat-traps in the yard and looking pretty light on his feet. Gary leaned over the fence and asked if he could help. He remembered Vandergelder's doglike yelp of surprise and pain as the trap sprung in his hand. Gary laughed without pleasure and tipped the coffee down the sink, squashed his feet into some crumbling sneakers. Out in the driveway, a couple of kids were stomping on the deck of his pickup. They gave him the finger.

—Your hair, man.

—Fucking spic.

Gary sighed and climbed into the cab. The kids jumped down, kicked the tires and lit Marlboros. Gary drove off down Aspen Boulevard. No aspens, just a few tired and dusty mimosas. Newdale Heights was a frayed fractal curve of suburban tract housing, about seventy miles from LA, that looked more half-erased than half-completed, thinly constructed identical bunga-lows in their own square of scrubby soil, surrounded by unmade hammerhead roads sketched in with broken curbing, littered with sacks of cement gone stiff years ago, and straggling twists of rusty cable. Gary swerved to avoid a dog sprawled in the road.

Remember being a kid here, he thought, actually sitting on the fucking porch with Mom and Dad. Like it was that old movie with that guy, Stewart Granger, *Have a Wonderful Life*. Unbeliev-able. Saying hello to folks without giving them the finger. Or raping their dog. Sitting on the porch in my short pants, forty years ago, with my hair slicked back. When there were fences.

13

His hand went to his hair, realizing what had triggered this bittersweet stroll down memory lane.

—Hair trigger, he said, for his own amusement. He fumbled for his aviator shades in the glovebox, and snarled at the rusty Jap cars on blocks in cracked driveways, the boarded-up windows, the sullen staring kids, the blurred knots of graffiti.

—Dick Van Dyke doesn't live here anymore. These guys do not have a fucking *idea* how to make the place look nice, I mean look at that fucking refrigerator, door hanging off, bust mattress, they sit out on that, their fat asses, dogshit all over.

Newdale Heights had started falling apart after the plant closed thirty years back. Then his dad had gotten sick, and his mom took off with the insurance broker who'd sold them the policy that was paying for his dad's care on the coast. Gary drove past the old plant, with its sagging cyclone fencing and peeling 'under development' sign. He'd painted a hyphen between the two words one night, secure in the knowledge that no one would understand why. Newdale was still behind the irony curtain. He made the right onto Main and stopped for the red light out front of Ed's Bait Shoppe. He peered up at the corroded bolt stubs that used to hold the big neon sign for Klub 45 way back whenever. The Hi-Tones had played more, or possibly fewer, gigs than he could remember at Klub 45. On Stage Tonite!!! Gary Wilder and The Hi-Tones ('Surferama') Plus Twist Contest!!! Newdale's Own!!! And afterward, swearing you could smell the surf a hundred miles away, with that little redhead wriggling in your lap, what was her name, Jenny something, nice tight ass . . .

He realized he was staring at a green light, and swung off onto Beach Street, pulling up in front of Wilder Sounds. The stores to either side were boarded up, but somehow Newdale's only guitar store had survived, and in a good year paid the grocery bills. He'd designed the sign himself, with letters like notes on a wavy stave. Across the street was the Your Favorite bar, where he and a bunch of other terminal under-achievers spent whatever time they could spare from their busy schedules, wondering why the waitress never threw any of them a fuck. Further down the road was the big mysterious Government Building, which someone long ago said was funded by the Defense Department to produce a new type of nerve gas, inspiring the Hi-Tones to pen an instrumental called 'Nerve Gas', which was eventually backed with 'Surferama', and a hit itself in some regions, when the jocks had enough sense to flip it. Whatever, it was a big mysterious building that employed mostly out-of-towners, and was probably an IRS office or something equally boring. Some way beyond that, and a tatty row of food stores selling strange vegetables from another planet, was a burnt-out drycleaner's and the trailer park, where Airstreams wobbled in the heat like mercury. Beyond that was the desert, where they kept all the rocks. Gary grunted as he bent to struggle with the lock on the shutter. Sweat ran off the end of his nose and made inky dots on the sidewalk. He went crosseyed looking at them.

—Yo, Gar . . .

He knew the voice. It was Carl, the skinny teenager who helped at the store. Gary lifted the shutter with a head-splitting rattle. He turned and wiped the sweat off his nose with the back of his hand. Carl was wearing a teeshirt with a design of a blown-apart chest. He pulled the front out so Gary could see it better.

—Neat, huh, Carl said, looking down at it. You can see all the organs and shit.

—Real educational. And your mom ironed it nice for you.

—Sucking Chest Wound Official Merchandise. He blew a pink bubble of gum. What's with the hair, Gar?

—Doo-wop. Big this summer, I swear truthfully.

Gary unlocked the door, cursing the worn-out key, and scooped up the mail. He waited for Carl to say something. He usually wanted something if he got in on time, Mondays most definitely so.

—Gar?

Gary raised an eyebrow, sifted through the mail, said nothing.

—Is it okay if I have the afternoon off?

—Little league commitments? Or seeing that fat old whore up at the trailer park?

—Got an audition.

—Great. Who for?

—Just these guys.

—Am I your fucking mom for chrissakes? Which these guys?

—Death Spasm.

Gary frowned. Do they play surf music?

—More thrash. Not really thrash metal. Death metal.

—Huh?

—Death thrash. Kinda. But with neat tunes.

Gary took his shades off and looked at Carl across the gulf of years.

—Whole world's a sucker for those neat tunes. Yeah, sure, kid. Rotsa ruck. Wanna borrow the amp?

Carl got stuck into the inventory with something approaching enthusiasm, and Gary sucked on a beer he'd taken from the icebox in the office. He stared up at his memorabilia corner, not for sale so don't ask and we mean it. A whole bunch of stuff hooked to some pegboard well out of reach. There was his first Mosrite, in cherry with a whammy bar, which he'd bought when The Wild Ones got their sponsorship deal from Hi-Tone Music Sales and had to change their name to The Hi-Tones. A faded peach satin sport coat with the name of their sponsor on the back, which he'd worn for the Battle of the Bands way out at Thousand Oaks. They'd come second to a bunch of longhairs who later mutated into Quicksilver Messenger Service and encouraged them to re-assess both their tailoring and their commitment to drug abuse.

Next to the sport coat, some old 45s, including the Wild Ones' 'Surferama' and 'Big Shot', on the old Regality label, which Gary knew were worth a lot of bucks to vinyl nerds. They did keep asking. And the sleeve to the only album they'd been on, the soundtrack to *Bikini Au-Go-Go*, a grade double-z teen-sploitation movie which featured an early line-up of The High in the party scene. The movie played at a few flyblown drive-ins but nobody noticed and everyone went back to their day jobs.

Soon after that, as The High, they started doing chemically induced three-hour versions of 'Nerve Gas', their hair started getting good in the back, and Hi-Tone Music Sales got edgy about the whole deal and withdrew their sponsorship. Gary remembered Arnie Cobb's concern over the name, The High. Wasn't there a danger of a connection with, you know, getting high on drugs? Gary had said well Arnie, there is a danger there, but hey, take a toke on this. Understandably, Arnie took the line that he didn't want the family business to be thought of as a head shop, kids wandering in off the street asking for roach clips. Gary caught himself snickering affectionately at the memory, getting all camply nostalgic. Suddenly he felt embarrassed about it. He turned to Carl and gestured up at the wall.

—What do you think about this stuff?

Carl looked up from a tray of plectrums he was counting. Huh? I lost my count.

—This old stuff. Think I should take it down?

Carl pursed his lips, thought for a moment. It's like history. I guess.

Yeah uh huh, thought Gary. It's like history. One day history is something only countries have and then whammo, you wake up to find you've got forty-six, no, forty-seven for God's *sake*, years of the stuff to call your very own. Half of which could be compressed into a single boring day without losing anything. He looked at his watch.

—I'll be in the bar if anyone needs me. Don't sell everything at once, huh.

He stepped into the shadeless heat just as a wretched-looking

17

tan compact scrubbed into the curb, popping a hubcap. Someone unfolded himself out onto the sidewalk and wiped his palms on his pant legs.

—Gary? he said, stretching his bony head forward on a razor-rash neck. His nylon shirt was a map of Sweatworld, showing major land masses and coastline detail. Gary felt suddenly clammy and nauseous. He hoped to hell he was wrong.

—Kent?

The man nodded, put his hand forward and snatched it back, wiping it on his thigh, put it forward again. Gary held it and shook it very carefully, in case it fell off. This was Kent Treacy, or someone doing a scarily good impression of what the guy would have looked like after being sandwashed in a Stasi basement for twenty years. A quarter of a century ago Kent Treacy had played guitar in The High, disappearing to Mexico to avoid the draft. He hadn't been heard of since, except for a postcard with suns drawn all over it. They stood staring dumbly at each other, Kent swaying slightly. Gary put his toe on the hubcap to stop it spinning.

—Shit, Kent, you've changed. Jesus. I hardly recognized you. If I'd known you were coming I'd have rented some majorettes.

Kent laughed, exactly the same laugh, a bit on edge, a bit crazy. He'd always been out of it, but back then he'd looked great, and now he looked sick. He pointed up at Gary's sign in mock surprise.

—Whoa! Hey, nice set-up you got here. Nice.

There was another silence. Gary could feel his guts tensing into a knot like a big slippery fist.

—Let me get you a beer, Kent? It's frying out here.

They crossed the street to the Your Favorite, Kent clapping his long hands like flippers.

—You've changed too, Gary. The hair. I didn't remember you at first. But me too, I guess, and it's been a long time. We'll do it right this time.

18

Do what right exactly? thought Gary, feeling like Death had just whispered his name.

—Well, we sure have a lot to talk about, Kent, he said, sounding to himself like some backslapping old shit with a nametag at a machine tools convention. They found a booth near the window where Gary could keep an eye on the store, and Cindy came over with her little pad and licked her pencil. She eyed Kent like he was a stain on the upholstery.

—And what can I get you gentlemen today? Hey, new *do*, Gary? The ribs are good.

—Just a couple beers, Cindy, said Gary, touching his hair selfconsciously. She'd always do that, you had a zit on your nose or you'd cut yourself shaving, she'd draw attention to it. He watched Kent watching her ass as she went back to the bar.

—So, Kent. Like her to lick your pencil?

Kent laughed, a little too loud. I sure would, Gar. That would be nice. I don't remember her. And this bar, too, I think, is new.

—Yeah. They just put it up fifteen years ago. We've had a whole bunch of presidents since you left. Keep getting it wrong. What brings you back to Newdale? Mexico all down to seeds and stems?

Kent rubbed his eyes with the heels of his hands. His fingernails were torn and dirty and his knuckles were skinned. His thin black hair scraped back in a ponytail held with a green rubber band.

—Well, Gary, you know, they got me good, and I did their time, man, I did their thing. I did that for them in Mexico city, man . . .

His voice did a dying fall. His eyes were watering, whether from being rubbed or crying Gary couldn't tell. Cindy brought their beers and they knocked the bottles together, like they used to. There was another silence. Kent didn't seem to be worried by it, looking round the place. Gary cleared his throat, sipped at his beer. Boy, I needed this. So, what brings you back to Newdale?

—My old man. Passed on. Put him in a box.

Kent blew his nose into a napkin, examined it briefly, folded it into his shirt pocket, just the red corner showing, like it was a dress shirt.

—I'm sorry. He was a nice guy.

Kent's face brightened, like someone had pulled a switch.

—But that's not why I'm here, man. This is a major trip. I'm re-forming The High, the greatest band, and there's a lot of interest in the psychedelic era right now, a lot of interest . . .

Gary slumped in his seat, weighing up the possibilities. He could shoot him through a seat cushion with the Colt Big Dave kept under the counter. He could feign a heart attack. He could stab him in the chest with a fork. He could just wave his arms and run yelling into the desert and never come back.

—Great idea, Kent.

—You think so?

—Sure, but talk to the others first, huh?

—Randy's dead, man . . .

—Uh huh. I heard that. Alex is in New York. Wife and kids. Got a gallery or something in SoHo. Talk to him. Bass player holds the whole band together.

Gary, awkwardly shifting his gaze into the street, noticed a guy carrying a guitar case into the store, and was grateful for an excuse to put a little space and thinking time between him and Kent. He jerked a thumb toward the store.

—Hey, excuse me, I got some business to attend to? I'll be right back . . . Cindy, another beer here?

Gary opened the door as the guy was opening the case. He was a short, thick-set, dark-haired guy in a creased suit and open-neck shirt. He had a heavy blue chin and Gary wondered if anyone had ever told him he looked like Fred Flintstone.

—This is the guy, Carl said, nodding toward Gary.

20

—What can I do for you, sir? said Gary cheerily.

—I think you may be interested in this.

He took an old blond-finish Fender out of the case. The needle on Gary's Hot Guitar Early Warning System flicked into the red. Early Tele? Broadcaster? He took the guitar carefully and examined the headstock.

—Is this what I think you think it is? This is a no-caster?

—A real live one from 'forty-eight. And here's the original factory receipt. Interested?

The so-called no-casters were the almost mythological, transitional models between Broadcasters and Telecasters while the name was under dispute. First time Gary had ever even seen one. Everything looked and felt exactly right. Well cared for, but used, and the wear was real, just as you'd want to see it. He handed it back to the guy and checked the serial number with a catalog he kept under the counter. Gary raised his eyebrows and prodded his chin with his thumb.

—Well, sir, I have to say this is the most interesting little item ever to walk into the shop on its own hind legs. But I need to speak to a guy I know before we can talk cash-style money, though. Give me a couple days? A day?

Fred Flintstone laid the guitar back in the scuffed plush-lined case. He stared down at it with his hands in his pockets.

—Listen, I need the money. Can't you make me an offer?

The guy's smile was a little fixed, a little glassy-eyed. Gary waited a couple of seconds.

—Well, I could, but it wouldn't be fair. This kind of thing is a little out of the ordinary, you know. I'd need to speak to this contact I have who's more of an expert value-wise.

—Okay, make me an offer based on what you know about the market.

Gary sighed. It looked like he was going to make some money in spite of his best efforts.

—I could make you an offer, but it would be low. I don't

want to have to auction it to turn a workable profit on the deal. Also it would have to be a check. We don't keep that kind of money in the cashbox.

The guy nudged the lock on the case with his toe, snapping it shut and open again.

—Okay. What kind of money are we talking about here?

Gary shrugged, eyeing the guy for his reaction. One, one and a half, that's my limit.

—One and a half grand?

—One thousand, five hundred, doll-ar-inis.

The guy looked down at the guitar, looked up at the ceiling. Looked out of the window, jingled some coins in his pocket. Looked at Gary.

—Make it cash and we got a deal.

Gary gave the guy one more chance.

—You'd make a better one if you waited a couple days.

It was Fred's turn to shrug. Gary went into his office and wrote out the check, and told Carl to run round to the bank and get the money. He gave him a Z-Mart bag to put it in. The guy was looking up at the stuff on the pegboard when Gary went back into the store.

—The Hi-Tones? I remember them.

—You live in the neighborhood? I'm gonna need some ID.

The guy gave Gary his driver's license.

—Thanks, Mr . . . ah, Leverton.

Gary felt strangely disappointed.

—Call me Ken. I used to come to that club on the corner here. Klub 45? Some wild nights. The things you do, huh?

—No kidding. They tell me I had a band there. Gary Wilder?

—Gary Wilder, right. And now this Wilder Sounds set-up. I wonder what happened to the rest of those guys.

—How'd you come by this little item, anyway? Gary said, to get off the subject of The Hi-Tones. The guy launched into a

22

long, rambling story involving his uncle and a jazz club in Pomona, and Gary gazed out into the street. A car swerved to avoid Kent Treacy, stepping off the curb in front of the bar. Gary heard the driver yell, Hey, fuckhead, but Kent seemed not to notice. Oh shit, thought Gary. Kent strolled over the road and rested his greasy forehead on the window, shading his eyes with his hands, staring into the store. Ken Flintstone was staring blankly up at the pegboard. Nothing happened for about a thousand years and then Carl burst through the door.

—I got it. He pushed the crumpled bag at Gary.

—Is it okay if I take the Marshall? My mom's coming by.

He noticed Kent, propped motionless at the window, forehead flattened into a white Zorro mask shape.

—Who's the flake?

Gary raised his eyebrows. Who he? A shadow out of time, and a terrible warning to the young, incidentally.

—Here's Mom.

Gary held the door open and Carl struggled the big combo out into the trunk of his mom's Chrysler. Gary counted out the money on the display case with the effects pedals in it, and had the guy sign the book. The guy rolled up the bills and snapped a green rubber band round them. Gary thinking, what is it with green rubber bands all of a fucking sudden?

They shook hands. The guy looked relieved. He turned at the door, snapping his fingers.

—I got it, he said. The Wild Ones, right? Gary Wilder and The Wild Ones?

Gary winked, made a pistol with his fingers, shot the guy with it.

—Wow, said the guy, shaking his head, Seems like yesterday, don't it? He sighed, ah well, and left with a catch-you-later wave. Gary shut the no-caster's case and took it into his office. No, today seems like yesterday, and probably tomorrow too, he

23

thought, but this is the best deal of my entire career in the music business anyway. Nice guy, too, for a cartoon character. A few thousand bucks for an hour's work. I can afford to take the day off. The month off.

Kent was still staring into the store as Gary left.

—You do all right, huh, Gary, he said quietly. Gary gently pulled him away from the window and rattled the shutter down.

—Uh, listen, Kent. I got a business deal in LA. I have to go, right? We can talk some other time?

Kent nodded seriously, pushed his fists into his pockets, scuffed across the sidewalk to his car.

—Sure.

They walked around the car, Gary realizing the motor was still running, had been all the time. Kent pulled the door open and creased himself into the driver's seat, tapping his fingers on the steering wheel. Gary shut the door gently and leaned down to look at him.

—You got any place to go? Anyone at home?

Kent turned and stared wide-eyed at Gary's chest.

—Barry Manilow, he said. But I got things to do. I'm seeing this guy from Oblivion Records. He wants The High reunion album. He wants to call it *Back To Earth, Down To Earth,* something . . . What do you think?

Gary gripped the door until his knuckles went white, fingers squeezing into the vinyl trim. It was hard to say what he thought today. It was all too much. The last thing he needed was to be part of some half-assed attempt to jump-start the corpse of a band that flatlined back in the vinyl era.

—I dunno, Kent. Talk to Alex. I haven't played in a band since we split up. I don't know. Things have happened to us, and it's not the same. Times change, you know?

—Alex. New York.

Gary patted him on the shoulder. Take care, Kent. And I'm

24

sorry about your old man. Drop by the house in a couple days and we'll catch up, okay?

Kent gunned the motor and took off up Beach Street, waving his big fin of a hand out the window. Gary watched him up past the Government Building, past the trailer park, way into the desert when the heat wobbled him off into the blue, like an Egyptian insect. He shook his head.

—Into the desert. Jesus Christ. What a day.

TWO

Gary's Night of Magical Love

Gary swung up into the cab of the pickup and headed out of town on the east road up into the hills. Twenty-five years. Where had Kent been? Why hadn't they talked about it? He felt weird, and it wasn't just the flashback of the acid-casualty housecall. Ken Flintstone and the pre-historic no-caster didn't help. Things like that should just never happen on a Monday morning. Mondays were strictly zoned for getting the bleak stuff over with, paperwork, bills, buying food, visiting his old man; leaving the rest of the week free for gaiety and petal-throwing. And his hair felt weird, his fucking hair, what was that about? He had to get away and let things settle down a little, sort his thoughts out.

A few miles out of town he made the turn-off up to the lake. A swim would clear the gunk off his hair and maybe out of his head. He remembered skinnydipping there, when they'd all been young and stupid and on good clean American recreational drugs. He remembered Marcie, her long hair and her laugh, and the flash of her skin as she dove off the jetty. That beautiful confident arc. Gary bellyflopping after, grabbing her ankle, clowning because he could never do something so beautiful, but Marcie pulling free and swimming strong out over the lake, leaving him behind, pretending to drown or something, knowing he could never keep up.

—Marcie. Jesus. Took the shower curtain and my Marvin Gaye albums. Left me talking to myself with a gunked-up head.

26

I'll be pushing a baby carriage full of newspapers next, listening to the voices in the plumbing with Kent Treacy. Go figure, she says. Eight years of marriage, you'd think we were an item, we'd got a stable base, and she walks. Okay, I'd been involved in a few unlucky business deals, so what, and she'd been right about the Argentinian groundnuts, what the fuck did I know about dirt and rain and shit, but she never let me forget it, rubbing my face in it all the time, and I'd just leased the store and things were starting to look good, took the Fender concession when Hi-Tone Music Sales folded, and she walks. What's a guy to do? Sure, there'd been complications, sex life had more downs than ups, but that constant criticism didn't help. Premature ejaculation, excuse me, premature for who exactly? And *yes*, I was a lazy slob. Intriguing facet of my roguish appeal. For fuck's sake, okay? If she couldn't see it as part of that whole bohemian vibe she'd once been part of, before she'd started picking her clothes off the floor and criticizing my friends, then that was her problem, right? And then glamor-boy, her new boss at the bank with the phony English accent and the superior smile and those fucking *shoes*, that time he came around. Just jangles the keys of the new branch in Oakland, and she walks. A bank, for Christ's sake, in Oakland. Well, I hope she's happy. No, actually, I hope she's so fucking miserable her ass crimps up, I really do, with her fucking shower curtain. Fuck her.

The narrow road became a dirt track between the trees, and the pickup bounced in the ruts. Gary braked by the creek, in the shade of a tree with their initials there somewhere, GW 4 MK, and walked up the path through the brush to the lake. The world was still and gleaming, the sky sprayed metalflake blue. He used what was left of the Private Property sign to climb over the barbed wire, like they'd always done, and stood looking down the grassy slope to the lake. It was enameled and perfect and guarded by glossy black-green trees, shoulder to shoulder. If he concentrated he could just hear traffic, thin and distorted with

27

heat, but here it was like a crystal paperweight, isolated and timeless. A row of small silver clouds hung above the trees like winged angel faces, waiting for a breeze. Gary had a quick look around to make sure there was no one making out in the long grass and strolled down to the water's edge, where an angled ledge of rock jutted out into the lake.

—That little bowl there in the rock, he said to himself, where we lit fires, huddled up passing joints round, I can taste it now, Randy that time tipping over backward off the edge, ah, Jesus . . .

He stripped off and hopped across the burning plate of dusty flat rock, falling into the waiting water, which folded up around him, heavy and bone-achingly cold. He punted out and floated face-down, corpse-like, watching the dimly waving weeds on the bottom.

—Somewhere down there is my Captain Midnight watch, and I will never get over her losing that. Big fat luminous numbers. I should never have let her fuck around with it. She can keep the shower curtain but I'd really like that watch back.

Gold-green spokes of sunlight wheeled slowly through the water, briefly igniting a patch of sand or a clump of dull weed in a gilded blur. A big dark fish turned, showing a soft gleam of slippery belly, and was gone amongst the weeds. Gary felt his back begin to fry, so he curled around, filling his lungs with cool air. He screwed his eyes shut against the sun, watched the pink and purple supernovas burst bloodily behind his eyelids, listening to his ears fizz.

—Made a few thousand buckarinis back there, boy, tell the guys, just in a day's work. Maybe buy them a drink. Yeah. No. Fuck 'em.

He edged his eyes open, filling his field of vision with candy blue. He remembered a helium balloon his mom had bought him when he was a kid, shiny blue against that same sky, that very same sky, tugging at the string.

—It wants to go, Mommy, it's pulling the string.

And letting it go, full of wonder and envy and love. Something wants to go, let it. He'd felt good watching it fly up into the sky like that, like it was a piece of him. He'd turned to his mom, proud that it was his balloon up there, wanting her to share in it. She'd jerked his arm real hard and bawled him out for wasting her money.

—Women, huh. Still up there somewhere maybe, and Captain Midnight on the bottom.

He swam a leisurely sidestroke around the lake, feeling the water slide all over him. Swimming was surprisingly easy. Effortless.

—I'm fitter than I thought. They do say these are the fittest years of your life, it's a medical fact, and you don't need to exercise or do shit, it's just natural. I am one fit fuck.

A jeweled green bug hovered in front of him, sounding like static on a tiny oriental radio, and slanted off in inscrutable geometry. Gary dove under the water and flipped over, looked up at the dimpled quicksilver mirror of the surface, and popped right back up like a cork. He rubbed his hair until it squeaked, getting the gunk well out of it, and swam back across the lake. He pulled himself up easily onto the flat rock, caveman prints, dawn of time, and lay naked in the itchy grass with his shirt over his head.

He thought vaguely about Kent, about how he didn't really understand his reactions to his turning up like that. He'd maybe have felt more emotional about it if it had been the same Kent he'd known ho-hum years ago; tan, skinny chick on his arm, but the guy that pulled up to the curb out of the past had lost whatever it was that had made him Kent Treacy. Maybe. And Gary had enough ghosts in his life without Kent rattling the chains in his face. He fell into a deep sleep for just under two seconds and lurched awake in vertigo panic. He dried his head on his Barry Manilow sweat and pulled on his clothes, burning

29

his thumb on his belt buckle, and pushed back through the scrub to the pickup. Way in the distance he could see the freeway, like a chalkline snapped on the hill, and the secret semaphore of windshield flashes. And by the time he reached the pickup he could feel his damn hair floating around again.

—Shit, he said, checking in the cab mirror, what a fucking pansy. This is beyond a fucking joke, I swear to God.

He pulled all the junk out of the glovebox, found his faded International Harvester baseball cap and jammed it down on his head. His fringe floated around so he pushed it up inside the band. All the way home he avoided looking at his reflection. Back in the house he found a scissors in the bathroom cabinet and eased his cap off, watching his hair float up with it.

—Jesus fucking Christ. Okay. Enough.

He sheared a lump off his fringe, and watched it suddenly go limp and heavy in his fingers. He dropped it into the basin, poked it tentatively with the scissors. The hair on his head was still doing some kind of sinuous wavy dance.

—What the fuck? I mean what the fuck . . .

He cut some more off, evening up the fringe, and the same thing happened. As soon as it left his head his hair started behaving itself. He cut some more off, and kept cutting, watching it pile up in the basin. It took maybe twenty minutes, and he looked like . . . an astronaut. A Soviet. A mental patient. A Soviet astronaut mental patient.

—A new look for Gary Wilder, he intoned in his passable Dan Rather. Tired of the sportscaster look, Gary today surprised his friends by flushing his hair down the toilet, where it joined his whole fucking life, incidentally. I mean, let's not start sucking on my own dick just because some schmuck practically gave me a guitar. The high point of my business career, make the sort of money these poodle-hair rock stars snork up their foil sinuses in like maybe one second.

With nothing else to do, he went into the living room and

30

flipped through a pile of albums stacked against the wall, gave up trying to find something he wanted to hear, and slid into the scuffed naugahyde couch, rubbing his nose. He looked around the room, curling his lip.

—I hate my life. My life stinks, he said, with no real feeling, just because it was Monday and this was what he said. When he'd moved his dad out, and his mom flew away with old pencil-neck, Gary got rid of all their stuff, and later when Marcie left she took her stuff, a whole bunch of which was his stuff, incidentally, and he'd bought nothing *homely* since. The place looked and felt like rented. Just ever so very occasionally he'd clean the place up, coinciding with the number of times he'd brought a date home, so not too much recently, but cleaning it for himself seemed like a waste of time when he had to watch TV and get depressed, or drive to the Your Favorite and get depressed with a load of other guys who'd had the community spirit to turn off the TV and drive out and get depressed together. Not that that was their intent, of course, they wanted it to be like *Cheers*, but no-one could do the one-liners, so every night seemed like a bad rehearsal for the real thing. A bunch of stale-smelling guys with combovers getting just drunk enough to be embarrassing but not embarrassed, and wondering why their rough male charm failed to moisten Cindy's panty-hose. Must be a lesbian, right. The way she licked that pencil. She was taunting them. They knew what she needed.

He slapped his knees, feeling unaccountably lightheaded all of a sudden.

—Maybe that swim has rejuvenated the oxygen in my bloodstream or something, that can happen, it's what that hydrotherapy shit is all about.

He ran his fingers over the springy astroturf on his scalp, hunted for the phone in a pile of old magazines and dialed the Your Favorite.

—Hey, Cindy. Gary. Yeah. Listen, you do hair, right?

31

—I did hair, Gary. But right now I work in a bar, right?

—But you used to do it?

—In Lancaster, yeah. Gary, I got customers . . .

—Did you ever see hair that kind of floats around? Not just sort of light, but kind of weightless?

—What, like flyaway hair? What are we talking about? What . . .

—Flyaway hair, right, and that happens overnight?

There was a pause, and Gary heard someone shout Cindy's name.

—Gary, I really do have to go, honey. Try to get some rest, okay?

She hung up. Flyaway hair. Maybe that was it. He'd seen ads. There was stuff you got from the pharmacy. He found the remote down the side of the cushion and fired it at the TV. The news dateline swam into focus.

—Shit. It's Monday, it's still Monday.

Monday nights, to complete the empty ritual of the day, to give him some fake impression of family quality time and add a bit of structure to the week, he drove out to the Buena Viva Care Center near the point to see his dad. Or someone who looked like him. His old man had Alzheimer's, and Gary hoped Alzheimer had his, the fuck. They hadn't had a rational conversation in ten years. Not that they'd been startlingly rational communicators before, of course, but ironically, i-*ron*-ically, they'd just learned to treat each other with a bit of grudging human respect when the shutters came down. There'd been moments since when the sunlight broke through the clouds, and the old guy wept in recognition and apology, clasping Gary's hands in his, but no more. Now he was represented by a loose and cynical sketch of a man which fooled nobody. Gary wondered where his real dad had floated off to, and if he knew about the rattling puppet he'd left behind, with its ventriloquist eyes and sly non-sequiturs. Now, once a week, Gary sat in front of him, looking at his watch, out the window, at a magazine, anywhere but at those dead rolling eyes, and he talked to the nurse, and then he drove back to the bar and Cindy'd ask how his old man was, and he racked up points for being the good son.

Gary groaned and made the effort to change into some pressed slacks, the only pair he kept on a hanger, which was the same as pressed, a clean shirt, and his Weejuns, and drove out through Newdale onto the freeway. It was two hours' drive, and as usual he couldn't remember a damn thing about it as he pulled into the Buena Viva. He could have been abducted by aliens for a total body cavity search for all he knew. The Buena Viva had been a motel a few years back, with a bad drugs rep. Now the drugs were all clean and legal and no fun at all. Stuccoed cabanas and gardens bright with flowers, and glittering lawns aerated by zimmerframes. There was a fake cannon out front and Gary wondered if they could use it to fire the stiffs into the ocean, save on burials. Every resident had a gilt-framed photograph of the Cordilleras, and grabrails round the toilet, and if there was any slapping around going on you never heard about it.

Gary found his father in the residents' room, perched on the edge of a couch with his head on one side as if listening for something. He was dressed in his brown wool sport coat and mustard slacks, and his hair had been neatly combed. Gary sat so he could look out between the scissor-cut silhouettes of the palms to the ocean.

—Hello, Dad.

Mr Wilder made a little insect sound at the back of his throat.

—Still circling the drain, huh, Dad?

The old man leaned forward conspiratorially and tapped his son's knee with a bony forefinger.

—Indians. I've been counting them.

Gary shifted uneasily in his seat. Indians, right. You been eating your meals?

An attempt to get back to the script. His dad chuckled.

—Fucking assholes, he said, little Indian faces.

He pulled an oven mitt from his pocket. Gary went to take it but his dad snatched it back. He really didn't need this today. He needed to be on a yacht somewhere with a hot little babe in a string bikini with his dick in her mouth, maybe no bikini . . . maybe just the top, pulled down a little . . .

—Everything okay, Mr Wilder?

—Huh? Gary flinched. It was Henry, the male nurse who cared for his dad most of the time. A quiet, attentive young guy with bad skin and piercing blue eyes. Gary could never figure the guy out. Why he was called Henry, what he was doing here, why he had cuffs on his pants . . .

—He's talkative today, isn't he? said Henry, turning to the old man. We're having quite a chat, aren't we, Mr Wilder?

—Is he eating okay?

—He enjoyed that chocolate cake you brought him, didn't you, Mr Wilder?

—He could use a shave.

—We tried, we tried. Some days he just wants the beard. Can I get you a coffee?

—No, thanks, Henry.

Gary stood up, fished in his pants pocket for a crumpled bill and pressed it into Henry's top pocket.

—Make sure he gets his vitamins. And he needs a button on his shirt. And he's got an oven mitt from somewhere.

—You really don't need to do this, Mr Wilder . . .

—Yeah, I know. Thanks, Henry.

His dad angled his head up. Lots of little Indians.

—I've got to go, Dad. Let Henry give you a shave. You look like a bum, for chrissakes.

Mr Wilder looked back over his shoulder and laughed politely at some joke he'd heard forty years ago, narrowing his eyes to slits. You could see his pupils flicking left and right. It made Gary feel queasy. He thanked Henry again and walked out past the front desk.

—Mr Wilder? It was the brunette on the desk.

—Terry. Hey. I'm sorry. Jesus, I was miles away. Hey, how are *you*?

She flashed him a smile. Gary's secret agenda at the Buena Viva.

—I'm good. I like your hair.

He put his hand to his head, embarrassed.

—Ha ha. Yeah, my hair. Bit of a change, I guess. The old man didn't recognize me. Ha ha again. Didn't recognize me?

—I like it. Kinda Charles Bronson, you know?

She tapped a gold-colored ballpoint on her white teeth and looked him in the eyes. What the hell, thought Gary. Today may be the day.

—How's, uh, Ben? Ken?

—Jerry? Yick. Don't even mention that jerk.

He felt his heart up the beat a little.

—Oh yeah? Well, how about mentioning dinner tonight?

Terry laughed. Why not? Thought you'd never ask.

—Pick you up at eight?

—Sounds neat. Here we go . . .

She wrote her address on the corner of some film star magazine she was looking at and tore it off, trying very hard indeed to keep the tear a straight line, concentrating with her head tilted to one side. Gary took the shiny triangle and interpreted the curly writing. She lived in a condo out at Elwood.

—Do you like seafood? said Gary, tucking the corner in his wallet.

—I just adore it . . . hey, there's the phone.

—Catch you later.

Out in the lot Gary did a discreet airpunch, keeping his elbow tucked right in.

—*Yesss*, he hissed, *you* still got it. Atta-fucking-*boy*.

He checked his watch and saw he had a couple of hours or so to kill, wondered if he should buy a new watch strap, or if an old scuffed one was more classy, kind of heirloom thing. The early evening was soft and scented, tasteful art colors in the sky. He pulled himself up into the cab of his pickup, and surprisingly shot right up like a rocket, cracking his skull on the edge of the roof. He buckled up, collapsed onto the asphalt and held his head.

—Ow, fucking *ow*, right. Jesus.

He got up, hoping Terry wasn't looking. He felt strangely light on his feet, balance shot. He climbed carefully into the cab, waited a minute, and drove slowly up the coast road, feeling the top of his head. No blood. Nothing he could see in the mirror. How the hell had that happened? And he still felt weird, swaying a little in the seat. He began to think about Terry.

—Should have asked months ago. Never had the confidence or something. Must get me some personal requisites from the pharmacy, up the back road a way, I think. That Trojan's been blistering my wallet since the Superbowl. The first one.

He tapped out the rhythm of 'Nerve Gas' on the steering wheel.

—Re-form The High. Terrible idea. Re-form The Wild Ones, slightly less terrible. Could do a few dates along the coast, supperclubs, hotel residencies. *Na na na-na dahhh, na na . . . n-n-n-nerve gasssss . . .* that stutter thing way before The Who, incidentally, limey fags, couple years. Live on stage tonite *and* in person, Newdale's finest, put your hands together for Larry and the Mild Ones . . . Jesus, that jerk. Larry and the fucking Mild Ones. On the flyer too.

He leaned out the window to check out a cute secretary driving home in her LeBaron. The sun was a soft maraschino cherry in a blue cocktail sky put there for him to bite with his big white handsome teeth. He began to realize that this weird

36

feeling was actually a great feeling. A bit like when you learn to let go when the acid hits. He felt crazily great. Did I take something? That bang on the head? Contact high with Kent Treacy? He checked his looks in the mirror.

—Kinda young, kinda wow. I do so look younger, too. The hair, sure, but less lined, a bit rounder, I dunno. Like Charles Bronson with tucks.

He pulled off the road and parked by a payphone blister on a pole. This little stretch of coast was usually empty, too rocky for the babes to pose comfortably and not enough surf to tilt a styrofoam cup. A big corroded pipe jutted out into the ocean from a lump of concrete. There was some rusty gym equipment on a square of broken cement, and Gary strolled to the gym bars and did a few chinups. The bars were sticky with salt. It was suspiciously easy. Usually he'd be struggling after five, but he just kept going for about fifty, until he lost count. He dropped down, wiping his hands off, thinking pretty damn good for an old guy though I do say so myself, and ducked under the plexiglass bubble over the payphone. He looked in his wallet for Paul French's business card and dialed the LA number. He was ready for the answerphone, waited patiently while Paul did his schtick over Deep Purple's 'Smoke on the Water' in the background.

—Paul, you wretched fuck, it is I. Gary, Gary Wilder, and I have some wood and wires you'd give me your ten-year-old daughter for, and her rollerskates. Call me. Ciao.

He sat on the edge of the cement square and looked at the ocean for a few minutes, feeling vaguely and routinely bitter about Paul French. A kind of equipment manager for a couple of big rock groups, wearing this loose-structured Italian suiting and a crack-head ponytail. Called himself an Interface Consultant to the Music Industry, right there on his card. Gary had told him it should be In Your Face Consultant but he hadn't laughed. The rich irony of his having been The High's road manager for a short

37

time – when they could afford it – was everpresent in Gary's mind.

Occasionally Paul would take something interesting from Gary for the guitar collectors in the bands, with a nasty aftertaste of having done the sad fuck a favour. Gary hated those fucking groups, all spray-on technique and pet beautician hair and no soul, no excitement, no *fun*. Not that you can talk to these snotty kid musicians anyway, you always had to speak to some shit-heel who called himself an Interface Consultant carving himself a piece of the action, protecting the artiste from losers like Gary. Sometimes he looked at Paul, networking for success, and thought, yeah, that's what he should have been, a roadie in the sixties instead of a pop star, and then he'd have had some kind of career path and a Dodge Viper that made women come just to look at it instead of a Japanese pickup that made them puke. He shuddered.

—But today is different, he said to himself. It's a whole new wonderful me. He watched the ocean for a couple more minutes, turning vague trivia over in his mind to no effect, and got back into the pickup. He drove slowly up toward Elwood, taking the back roads and scowling at the scenery. Development was strung out all along here, making it impossible to tell where one town stopped and another began. He passed a row of small stores with those dinky mansard roofs that were all over the place, apparently just fell out the sky overnight. Frogs 'n' Stuff. The Gourmet Candle Shoppe. Who the fuck went to these places? Herb World. The Cuteness Cottage. Nobody cared about selling commodities to Gary Wilder anymore. Whole communities based around stuff he'd never want. They should have signs up – Nothing For You Here, Gary.

The pharmacy didn't have a Rubbers 'n' Stuff sign yet but it was only a matter of time. He pulled up and went inside. It smelt like a grandmother's purse in there. An old guy with carefully combed white hair and union-supplied wireframe glasses was reading a newspaper spread on the counter. He didn't look up as the little bell above the door tinkled. Gary idly picked up a clear yellow plastic toothbrush and a packet of rubbers from the rack on the counter.

—Got anything for flyaway hair?

The old guy looked up, his gray eyes twinkling.

—Bit late, isn't it? Looks like yours took off already. He laughed politely at his own joke.

—Yeah, well, I hope you never have to go through chemotherapy. It's not as amusing as you seem to find it.

—You might try that can behind you, sir. Middle shelf. HairMuscle for Men. The Gym in a Tin. Ought to do the trick.

Gary didn't take his eyes off him. Yeah? Maybe not. I'll just take these.

The guy put the toothbrush into a paper bag.

—You know this is a child's toothbrush?

—It's a gift, said Gary. The old guy dropped the rubbers into the bag. For after she gives me oral sex, continued Gary. Incidentally, those rubbers any good? He flicked a ten-dollar bill on the newspaper and the guy gave him his change without saying anything, but his cheeks were bright red and his eyes hard as buttons. On the way out, Gary stood on the scales by the door, curious.

—Are these right?

The guy slowly unhooked his glasses and pinched the bridge of his nose. Meaning what, exactly?

—Meaning do they weigh right, I guess.

—Don't shoot the scales, sir. They're just doing their job.

Gary looked at the dial again, jiggled a little on the footplate. The needle settled to a hundred and ten pounds.

—Well, if they're right, something is seriously weird. What do I look to you, two hundred? More?

The guy looked back at his newspaper.

—It was on account of not making any money in the guess-your-weight business that we bought the scales. Times are hard.

—Specially since Rockwell's checks stopped coming in, huh? said Gary, opening the door and making the little silver bell tinkle. Incidentally, those rubbers better make her squeal like a little pink pig or I'm bringing them back.

The De La Mer was the coast's premier seafood eatery. Gary knew this because it said so on a pink and blue neon sign. He'd been here before, years back, but didn't remember it like this. Inside it was like a terrible collision between a Puerto Rican whorehouse coming in from one direction and a giant Jewish aquarium coming in from the other, and some Hawaiian on acid had tried to clean it up. A waxy-looking guy who looked like he might burst into tears made a reservation for him at a desk with a lime-green plastic scallop lampshade, and he went to the mensroom to freshen up. The underwater theme had been carried through to the urinals, which were like pink shells, reinforcing Gary's belief that a homosexual cabal had completely infiltrated the restaurant industry. Someone in the john was whistling the theme from *Bewitched*. The mirror was encrusted with orange styrene coral, and he barely recognized himself in it. His face was rounder somehow, and with the flattop he looked a good ten years younger.

—Why, you dog, he said suavely, all those years of clean living paying off, but weird for sure, some kind of glandular boost, maybe, and look at this for chrissakes . . .

He lifted himself off the floor with his hands on the basin rim, but startlingly easily, his feet coming up behind him. He felt some kind of tingling rush in his bloodstream, and before he knew what was happening he was doing a handstand, his toes touching the ceiling. Loose change fell from his pockets and bounced on the tile floor. The door opened and a guy with blue-white hair and a lavender-colored leisure suit with LA-pels stood looking at him, astonished. Gary's mind went blank. He could think of absolutely nothing to say.

—This is not a gym, sir, said the guy in the lavender suit after an interval, and backed out.

Gary felt his arms aching and he collapsed, scattering the cologne and the towel basket. He sat on the floor, scooping up the dropped coins automatically, for something to do. Something simple he could understand. He got to his feet very slowly, gripping the basin. He felt okay, he guessed. What the fuck had happened? He did some deep breathing and walked slowly into the bar, with a definite spring in his step. So definite, in fact, it felt like walking in chest-high water. He peered accusingly at the floor. Had they put rubber tiles in or what? He anchored himself to a barstool and ordered a martini, no ferns, lots of ice. There was plenty of time to get straight, deal with this thing. Terry's condo was maybe ten minutes' drive. The barman placed his glass on a pink paper shell. Gary felt the peculiar rush again, like his bloodstream had just been carbonated.

—Wow, and I didn't even drink it yet.

—Sir?

—Nothing. I just feel a little, lightheaded, something. Hey, this place has changed since I was here last. What happened to Martine?

—New demographic, the barman said, nodding toward the guy in the lavender suit, who was frowning at Gary from the other end of the bar.

Gary frowned back. The twinkie? That's . . . uh, Martine?

The barman pouted and polished some glasses with a big floppy white cloth.

—Well, pardon me all to heck, said Gary under his breath. He swallowed his martini and got off the barstool, catapulting himself across the room, spiraling crazily through the air toward a table ten feet away. He bellyflopped amongst the hors d'oeuvres

41

and the couple sitting there leaped to their feet, knocking their chairs over, the woman stifling a scream with her napkin. Gary, dazed and confused, eased back off the table, bringing the cloth with him. There was the sound of breaking glass and scattering cutlery. He wiped some salty slime from his face with the back of his hand. There was stuff all over his shirt and jacket, and he was having a lot of trouble with his balance.

—What the fuck? he said, in a voice strained with surprise.

The restaurant was now very quiet, and very still. The guy standing back from the table was desperately looking around for assistance, trying to say something, his mouth opening and closing, a big dumb fish. In a moment of insane calm Gary noticed that the guy's red face stopped in an exact straight line where his baldness began, like he was wearing a tight white rubber bathing cap. The lavender suit came over, breaking the spell of silence by snapping his fingers for a waiter.

—What seems to be the trouble here?

—This, this . . . began the bald guy, flapping a napkin at Gary.

—Did you see that? Gary said hoarsely. Fucking springs in the barstool. He stabbed an accusing forefinger at the barstool.

—I'm afraid we must ask you to leave, sir.

—Jesus fucking Christ. This is my good shirt.

—That's *enough*. Clark? Where's Clark?

Gary was still trying to get his balance, his arms out to either side like a tightrope walker. Someone shouted, throw the drunken bum out. A couple of waiters began cleaning up the mess, and conversations started up. Everyone was looking at him like he was hot cat vomit.

—I may sue, said Gary, weaving toward the door. Something is definitely a little wrong here, he thought. I can hardly touch the floor. Am I drunk or what?

An unsmiling waiter held the door open for him, avoiding eye contact, and he tiptoed uncertainly down the steps.

—Something in that martini.

He grabbed the tubular steel handrail and gulped in the warm night air. A couple coming in looked at him strangely, backing away.

—Don't drink the martini, he said, in a higher voice than he'd intended. He tried to take a step down and lost his balance or slipped without his foot touching anything. His legs flailed up as he grabbed the rail and he wrapped himself around it, clinging to it like a sloth. His loose change fell out of his pocket again and clinked down the steps.

—What the fuck? . . . Fuck . . .

The doors opened and the manager came out, followed by two blond waiters.

—Jimmy, Clark, he said. Make sure this gentleman gets to his car.

—Don't you fucking Nazis even *touch* me, you fucking . . .

—Or we simply telephone the police if you prefer.

—I can leave without your help, thank you. *Jesus.* Let me get my breath, willya . . .

He unhooked his legs from the rail and pedaled his feet slowly to the ground, twisting around with the rail behind him, pulling up on it to keep his feet on the deck.

—I'm okay, really. Look. Just give me a minute. I'm fine.

—We don't want any more trouble, you understand, sir.

—Hell, me neither. I'm out of here.

He took a step down, and another, pulling up on the rail all the time.

—I guess I won't be needing that table later, he added helpfully.

He reached the last step and turned to see the lavender suit and the waiters go back inside. The pickup was twenty feet away. He steadied himself and let go the rail. He felt okay. He took a step. Fine. A little wobbly, maybe. Strong drink on an empty stomach, understandable. The walk to the pickup was the longest he'd taken since he'd walked to Mars that time in 'sixty-nine. His clothes were soaked in sweat. He opened the door and eased himself up into the cab, cracking his head on the roof again, in exactly the same spot. His feet splayed up and out behind him and he grabbed the steering wheel, pulled himself inside, hooked his heels under the seat, hugging the wheel to his chest.

He sat like that for maybe five minutes before shutting the door. His thoughts were chaotic, multi-layered. Moments of deceptive normality swamped by great nauseating waves of clammy panic, confused with vivid replays of the day's strange encounters. Kent. Stunt hair. Kent again, wiping his palms on his thighs. Laughing. Terry. Doing those chinups with no effort. Swimming across the lake with no effort. Flying across the restaurant with no effort. All these events were telling him something. They were telling him something stupid, wrong, and impossible, and he didn't like it. He stared at the twisted, desperate face in the cab mirror, with its strange hair and stranger's eyes.

—This is not so great, he said. He buckled the seatbelt across his lap, pulling it tight, and headed for home, torturing himself with thoughts of his date with Terry. Every time he passed a phonebooth he slowed, thinking he should maybe phone her with some kind of excuse, but he just couldn't think of one, and telling the truth didn't seem a viable option. I can't make it tonight because I've started floating around, yeah, kind of like an astronaut or something, how about that. Crazy, huh? No, I'll be okay, I'll phone you in the morning, thanks for being so understanding.

He drove slowly, like an old guy looking for an address, pushing himself into the seat, arms straight against the steering wheel. From time to time he got a kind of sinking feeling in his stomach, like you get in an elevator, and he felt his weight press down, and everything seemed normal again, and he'd almost turn around to pick Terry up, surfing on a great wave of relief.

No way any of that had actually happened for real. And then a moment later he'd get that fizzing rush in his blood and feel the seatbelt tighten across his lap. Steering was especially difficult, as turning the wheel had the effect of twisting him around in the other direction, so he jammed his knees under the dash. He kept gear changes and braking to the minimum, and wasn't exactly surprised when, at the bottom of the offramp for Newdale, he saw a blue gumball flash in the cab mirror. He pulled over just as they blipped the siren. He wound down the window, squeezing his thighs up against the wheel, and watched the cop approach in that all-the-time-in-the-world way they have, making important little notes in an important little notebook. Shitfuck, thought Gary.

—Hello, officer.

The cop folded his night-driving shades and hooked them on his breast pocket, remaining stonily impassive, like the manual says.

—Can I see your registration and your license, please, sir.

This was not spoken as a request. Gary showed him the paperwork.

—Anything wrong, officer?

—Anything wrong with your brights?

It was now pretty dark, Gary noticed suddenly. He slapped his forehead with the palm of his hand, and twisted the stem switch.

—Eee-yow. I guess I forgot.

—I guess you did, sir. Have you been drinking any alcohol this evening?

Please don't ask me to get out of the cab, thought Gary.

—Just a martini at the De La Mer. Which I don't recommend, incidentally. Ha ha.

—I see, sir. The De La Mer. Would you get out of the cab, please.

Gary's mind swerved like a top about to keel over. I'd rather not, really.

45

The cop took a step back. Just get out of the cab.

—There's a reason, I mean my driving, and lights. I'd really rather not get out. It's kind of embarrassing.

—Uh-huh. What's the problem?

Gary had a flash of inspiration and dropped his voice to a hoarse whisper.

—It's just that I've shit myself. Got a bug or something, feel terrible. I live in Newdale? I really need to get home and shower, clean out the cab. Really, that martini didn't help.

The cop looked back to the patrol car, tapped his pencil on his notebook, face like Mount Rushmore.

—Hey, Jerry, he yelled. Guy here shit hisself.

—You do have that effect on folks, Dennis, for sure, the cop in the car shouted back.

Dennis handed Gary's license back at arm's length.

—Okay, you better take off. Don't drive if you're sick, huh? He walked back to the squad car, shaking his head.

Gary leaned out the window. I'm serious about that martini. The FDA should check that place out. The De La Mer out at Elwood.

A little later, Gary pulled into his driveway during a reassuring period of normal weight. He jumped from the cab and stomped on the concrete, strangely aware of the weight of his body hanging from his bones by a knotty, gristly, creaking web of muscle and ligament.

Maybe that's it, then, over, he thought. Whatever it was, maybe I'm okay.

He let himself in the back door and threw his clothes off on his way to the bedroom, letting them lie where they fell, in a sleazy parody of the clichéd tracking shot to the lover's naked embrace. He fell into the stale empty bed like a bear into a pit.

THREE

My Little Problem

Gary struggled up out of the rooty tangle of his dreams mumble-mouthed and slimy with sweat, shreds of bloody shouting stuff slipping off somewhere. It was dark and hot, and there was something pressing on his stomach. Bits of yesterday fanned up into his head, shuffled with highly colored dream segments, not quite interlocking. He struggled to sort them out, working his tongue around the sharply dry cave of his mouth. What had that been about? Was this a dream or a memory? He cleared his throat, rubbed his cropped head. That was real enough. He felt the thing on his stomach. A big cool globe on a metal rod. Familiar. He reached out to turn on the lamp, and his arm waved in empty space, clutching at nothing. Then his heart started to bang in his chest like it was trying to jump up his throat. There was nothing beneath him. Nothing but air. Sweat dribbled off his clammy sides, icewater veins. He grabbed the globe on his stomach. It was the ceiling lamp. This was the ceiling lamp. He could feel the screwheads you undid to get at the bulb, one missing. He tried to calm his hammering heart, clinging there to the ceiling lamp.

—Calm, be calm, be still . . . What was that mantra? Ma padne dal . . . shit . . . pa mad . . . fuckshit . . . fucking mantra cost me twenty bucks, Kent Treacy, you son of a bitch . . . oh, fucking Jesus help me . . . oh fuck . . .

He curled around the lamp, with his head and knees against

the chalky ceiling, watching dustmotes igniting in a copper blade of sunlight between the curtains.

—I really have to come to terms with this shit. I really do, he said aloud, and with a massive effort of willpower he let go of the lamp and gently pushed up at the ceiling with his hands and feet. He floated down slowly, like soap in the tub, and grabbed at the bed beneath him, tight fistfuls of twisted sheet.

—Okay. Okay.

He sat up, pushing his legs under the sheet as an anchor. It didn't seem to need much to hold him down.

—Maybe it's not me. Maybe it's everything else getting heavier. Maybe Kent put an old Mexican hex on me. Mex hex. Started earlier, all that shit with the hair. I really need some-body's help here.

He reached for the cord from the bedside lamp and snapped the switch. First thing he did was check that the big globe lamp was still on the ceiling, he hadn't hallucinated it. He looked at the clock by the bed, one of those early digital Radio Shack deals with the flopover numbers.

—Seven twenty-eight, twenty-nine. Who can I wake up and talk to about this?

He went through an inventory of everyone he could possibly talk to. He'd have to get somebody to come around, use some kind of excuse. Making the list in his head, the discipline of it, helped to calm him down. He spoke aloud, keeping his voice even.

—Okay. We got Big Dave at the Your Favorite. Cynical bastard, not exactly sympathetic. Bobby at the Your Favorite. My buddy Bobby. Sold that Les Paul Special I virtually gave him, one day later, made four hundred bucks, the shit. So. We got Ray at the barbershop, nice quiet guy, kept an eye on the house that time I went east. Ray Gregory, definite possibility. Dan. Dan Elmore. Don't know his home number. Don't know

48

anybody's home fucking number. Phone my dad . . . my mom . . .

He suddenly felt a huge wave of childlike loneliness crash over him and he started to cry uncontrollably, great heaving sobs hurting his chest they were so big. He sat on his big grownup bed and cried until his eyes stung, until nothing else came but shudders, and his nose ran, but he wouldn't let go the sheets to wipe it. Then he stopped, as suddenly as he'd started, sniffed horribly, and spoke aloud in a very calm voice.

—I am as hungry as fuck. I do know that much. Jesus. I didn't eat in twenty-four hours. More. Need something heavy in my stomach. Pizza. Send out for a pizza, Four Seasons, extra everything. Forgot to eat, sure I feel weird, effect on metabolism, side effects.

Gary looked apprehensively at the vast distance to the door. The gloomy cathedral of his room. It was like learning to swim, going out of his depth for the first time. He let go with his right hand, fingers hurting from being clenched so tight, and brought his legs up and around, counteracting the tendency to roll over backward with his arms. He crooked his legs under the bed, bracing his feet against the carpet. Then he very gently stood up, keeping some tension between the bed behind his knees and his feet on the floor. He stood like that for some time, breathing deep and slow to calm his heartbeat.

—Okay, okay. Just a little step here. One small step for man, one . . . whoa . . .

He'd left the ground, curling over slowly, hands out in front like a diver. Then he found himself doing a handstand, while his body and legs kept going back over him. It was all very slow and dreamlike, and Gary was surprised by the calmness of it. He rolled over in mid-air, watching the room turn upside-down, came over just in time to grab the dresser, bring his feet down, hook his toes under the drawer, come to a rest.

49

—This is a snap, he said, not really convincing himself. He opened the door, holding onto the dresser with his other hand, and looked across the hall to the living room, bright and normal in the morning sun, and the phone on the arm of the chair. Nice normal chair and phone. He started to cry again but immediately broke out in a stupid, desperate laugh. He bent over the dresser, hugging it to his chest, sweaty face pressed up hard to the dusty teak-effect laminate.

—This is not right, this is not right . . .

He held the position until his back ached, going through the arguments against any of this happening, having a sane and lucid conversation with himself about something totally unacceptable. This could not be happening, whatever it was, and that was all there was to it. Period. Some kind of mental thing, flashback. He peeled his face from the surface, making a sour grimace, trying to work up enough spit to swallow the dust. He stood up, all the muscles in his back like cardboard. Now it was only too obvious that it *was* happening, whatever it was. It seemed like days had gone by since he woke up, and he was exhausted.

—Okay, Wilder, he said quietly, deal with it.

He edged around the dresser until he was in a position to make a dive across the hall, and did a tentative little toddler's jump, getting both the line of approach and velocity wildly wrong. He flew up through the doorway, slewed around, and smacked into the ceiling with his arms and legs all over the place. He grabbed for the top of the door frame and braced himself across the hall, remembering a Bond movie where 007 had done just such a thing to get out of a jail cell. Again he waited while a panic attack subsided, unconsciously using a technique he'd evolved for bad acid trips, dormant now for a quarter of a century. Using his hands on the door frame, he swung down and stood in the doorway. He could feel a number of interesting bruises competing for his attention, but he had more pressing concerns. He'd never felt quite so hungry in his life, and thirsty

50

too. The phone on the chair was about six feet away, but it was six feet he didn't know how to make. He walked his hands down the sides of the door frame, finishing in a squat, and grabbed for the carpet, thanking Marcie for insisting on shag pile. He crawled across the carpet, pulling himself forward with fingerfuls of wool-nylon mix and knees hugged up under his chest, six inches at a time.

—Cost a fortune, incidentally, and it's filthy, look at this. I must get this cleaned, what's this, dog hair? Who has a fucking dog?

He made a grab for the sticky-feeling naugahyde chair arm and wedged a foot under the seat squab, fumbled with the phone, taking an anguished minute to remember the number.

—You've reached Dr McKernan's office. Consultation hours are . . .

—Holy shit.

He felt under the chair, found the crumpled notebook with the numbers penciled in, looked up the number, redialed, starting to panic again.

—Pizza Chateau, this is Clarice, how may I help you?

—Oh God, you're open, thank God . . .

—We provide a twenty-four-hour delivery service within the Newdale area . . .

—Yeah, and I love you for it, Clarice. This is 2233 Aspen. I need a Four Seasons, family size, extra pepperoni, extra olives, extra cheese, extra onions, no anchovies. Did I say extra cheese? Okay. No anchovies. And a bucket of fries, family size bucket of fries, and a large Coke. No anchovies.

—In the Coke?

—Anywhere.

He waited while Clarice read his order back, gum-chewing slow.

—Er, listen, Clarice, he said, something just occurring to him. Everybody okay there?

51

—Sure. Thank you. How are you? Have a nice day.

Have a nice day? Okay, it looked like it was just him, and not the end of civilization like in some science-fiction movie. Or maybe Pizza Chateau had managed to escape the effect somehow, and were oblivious to everyone else just flying off into space, an oasis of pizza-baking normality. Gary didn't think so. He put the phone back on the arm of the chair and wondered what to do next, before realizing he was floating naked in an uncurtained room in broad daylight. He combat-crawled back into the hall.

—Clothes. Next priority, put something on, easy, jeans, sweat, nothing formal. Hey . . . wait a second here . . .

He felt the elevator effect in his belly, and his butt cheeks spread as his weight returned, and then his breath went out of him like he'd been hit with a gunny sack. He struggled to his feet, feeling the strain on his legs and back, feeling like an old man. Every muscle and joint ached.

—Thank you, God and baby Jesus, thank you, thank you.

He felt like sobbing with relief. Was it over? Was he okay? But maybe it would come back? There was no telling how long this was going to last. He got dressed quickly, pulling on yesterday's jeans and a crumpled What, Me Worry? sweatshirt. Then he went out into the garage and started fumbling around in a pile of stuff that Marcie had somehow omitted to take with her. When the pizza came he answered the door wearing a weighted scuba belt he'd bought at a garage sale, steel-toed construction boots, and a backpack containing a small sack of cement. His veins were fizzing quietly. The delivery boy saw nothing unusual, this was California, and began his nasal recitation.

—*One* family Four extra cheese pepperoni onions olives anchovies *family* fries *large* Coke, nine ninety-five.

—Anchovies? What extra anchovies? I ordered no anchovies. Ixnay on the anchoviesay. Capisco?

52

The boy consulted the ticket on the pizza carton and repeated the text slowly, as if Gary hadn't quite understood.

—One family Four, extra cheese, pepperoni, onions, olives, *anchovies*.

He showed Gary the ticket. Gary sighed and gave him a ten.

—If there are anchovies in the Coke I will find where you live and push them up your nose while you sleep. Keep the change for your trouble.

Gary scarfed back his food in the kitchen, picking off the anchovies and flicking them into the sink. Feeling better, he belched twice, savoring the flavor. Why did they never do a Pepsi belch challenge? He loosened his diver's belt a notch and checked his watch. It was nearly ten.

—Shit, the store. Carl's on the sidewalk, sitting on the Marshall, rubbing his heels on the cloth.

He stood up, noticing a subtle change in his balance and trying to ignore it, like it was a dog humping his leg at a funeral. He felt a deep, nauseous feeling of sawing dread, like a barely heard horror movie soundtrack getting louder. He made fists to stop his fingertips trembling.

—Maybe it's just heartburn, he said, belching again. Anchovies poison what they're on, well known fact.

He slapped the table with the palm of his hand, suddenly impatient with himself.

—No no no, it's not the diet, not the lack of food, how the fuck could it be anyway, you sad fuck. Oh shit. Shit shit shit.

He stood up, took a few wobbly baby steps, swaying a little but nothing he couldn't handle. His centre of gravity was a little skewed, but with care he could get around okay. He went to the bathroom to take a piss, immensely reassured that it described the familiar arc into the bowl, and went outside to the pickup. One of the kids from across the road was leaning against the hood. Gary ignored him and climbed into the cab, squashing up against the wheel because of the backpack. He gunned the throttle. The kid slouched off, spitting generously on the driveway.

—What the fuck is it with fucking kids today? Where does he find the room in his tiny head for that pile of glop he just hacked up on my driveway? Jesus, when I take a dump I hope to God it's okay, normal weight, doesn't float around. I don't get this I honest to God do not get any of this whatso-fucking-ever I really do not.

Driving wasn't too much of a problem, and he pulled up at the curb outside the store to find Carl sitting on the Marshall rubbing his heels on the speaker cloth. He wound down the window.

—Yo, Carl. How'd the audition go?

Carl stood up and came over to the pickup, swung the bill of his baseball cap round to the back.

—It went good, I guess. They got a whole bunch of guys to try. I didn't need the amp. Blackie let me use his, which was like totally instantaneous, this real cool Mesa-Boogie?

Carl's fingers turned imaginary knobs in the air.

—Yeah, at least you gave it your best shot, huh. Can't do more.

Carl looked at Gary's hair quizzically.

—Doo-wop and now what? You going jazz on us? What's with the backpack?

—Uh, listen. I'm shutting the store for a few days, going to the mountains. I'll phone you.

—What about the amp?

Gary thought for a moment. He didn't want to get out of the cab and unlock the store and all that shit with a diver's belt and a full backpack on. Carl quite clearly already thought he'd gone a little postal.

—I'll give you a ride home with it. But don't rub the fucking speaker cloth, for fuck's sake. Look after it or I'll take it out your wages.

Carl grinned, and loaded the Marshall up on the bed of the pickup. On the way to his home, Carl looked at Gary strangely from the corner of his eye.

—What's up, kid? asked Gary, adding a mental reply of, Well, I am, actually.

—Are you okay, Gar?

—Sure I'm okay. Made a lot of money yesterday. I can afford a vacation.

Carl tapped his fingers on the dash, nodding his head to some interior beat.

—It's just, uh, the hair, you know, and, like, the diver's belt?

—Listen, said Gary, thinking fast, I'm going on one of those survival deals in the woods. We have to carry weights and climb cliffs and drink our own piss and shit. Real army stuff. That's why I cut my hair.

—Drink your own piss? Ee-yew. Gross me out.

This sounded so convincing, the cunning of the insane, that Gary believed it himself. Certainly Carl had seemed to, and he talked about the audition for the rest of the trip home. Gary wasn't listening. He was trying to work out what he was going to do. The weightless effect seemed to come and go in phases. Would they get fewer and weaker, or what? The possibilities, a poisoned word in the circumstances, seemed terrible. What if? What if? He had to let someone in on it. He'd need help. He needed help already. Again he went through everyone he knew, ruling them out for various reasons. And then he thought of Gretchen. She was discreet, at least. She'd never blown the whistle on Vandergelder, never badmouthed him. She was pleasant and quiet. And she lived next door.

—Uh, Gary . . . we missed it . . .

Gary did a three-point turn in someone's driveway, and drew up outside Carl's house.

55

—Enjoy your vacation, Carl said, after he'd lugged the amp down onto the sidewalk. I hope you don't get thirsty . . .

Gary could hear Carl's little sister yelling at someone in the house. He let the clutch out, catching a little rubber, and crossed two red lights on the way home without seeing them. Gretchen was just leaving Vandergelder's house as Gary pulled into his driveway. She pushed a stray strand of blond hair behind her ear, the car keys jingling like a massive African earring.

—Hey, Gary.

—Gretchen, hi. How you doing?

—Comme ci, comme ca. Going somewhere, or coming back?

—I wish I knew. Listen, Gretchen, can you spare a few minutes? Cup of coffee? I really need to, uh . . .

Gretchen put her head on one side. The stray lock of hair fell across her face again.

—Are you in some kind of trouble?

—It's that obvious? Yeah, some kind, I guess. Can we go inside?

—I really have to get to the mall, but five minutes, I guess, okay.

Gary swung down awkwardly from the cab. He could feel the weights working against the effect, warping his balance. He let them in the side door, and they went through to the kitchen. He dusted off a chair with a dishcloth and Gretchen sat down. She looked worried, picking up on his anxiety.

—What's happening, Gary? Are you in trouble with the police?

—Hell, no. He rubbed his face with the palms of his hands. It's like, Jesus, I . . . really, I don't know how to start. Maybe I shouldn't have asked you, I don't know. This is so stupid. Really. No, let's forget it.

—What is it, Gary? she said, frowning. Gary shook his head. They were silent for a while. Then Gary unbuckled his backpack.

—Watch, he said, just . . . watch.

He lowered the pack to the floor, holding onto the sink edge with one hand, and unbuckled his diver's belt.

—Okay, he said, no *way* you're ready for this.

He let go the sink, bent his knees, and rose gently, pushing back off the ceiling with his fingertips. The weight of his boots kept him upright. As soon as he touched the floor, he grabbed the table and swung his legs under. He couldn't help feeling a little proud of the gracefulness of the maneuver. He looked at Gretchen. Her mouth was open and she was entirely still.

—So, said Gary. My little problem.

He pulled a chair under him with the toe of his boot, and pretended to sit on it to make Gretchen feel more at ease.

—Wow, she said, just breathing the word. Wow.

—I know. What else can you say?

—Jesus Christ, Gary . . .

—That too.

—No ropes? Mirrors?

Gary shook his head. I wish it was that simple. It's kind of an effect. Comes and goes.

—Since when?

—Since yesterday, I think. Seems like years.

Gary went through everything he could remember happening to him since he'd noticed his hair in the mirror, right up to his lie to Carl about the survival camp.

—Want to do it again? said Gretchen, a little warily. Float around a little?

—Don't believe your eyes, huh? Still think it's a trick?

Gary did pretty much the same sort of maneuver, this time losing his orientation during the descent, and his windmilling arms scattered the saucepans on the stove. Gretchen instinctively bent to pick them up. Gary watched her, getting angry for no reason he could think of.

—Leave them, for fuck's sake, Gretchen, leave them . . . it doesn't matter . . . fuck the saucepans . . .

57

Gretchen froze, her head down, looking at a skillet in her hand.

—Fuck, said Gary under his breath. I'm sorry, Gretchen.

She looked up. She looked as if she was about to hit him with the skillet.

—Don't be so . . . *caustic*, Gary. It doesn't help. You need help. This is, I don't know, kind of horrible. You're not . . . this doesn't . . . it's not right. You . . .

Gary was tensed between the stove and the table. He angled himself around and twisted his legs around the table legs. He felt stupid and ashamed and helpless.

—I'm sorry, Gretchen, he said. I'm really sorry. I don't know what's happening to me.

Gretchen's face softened. She held her face in her hands.

—You still want that coffee? You're really in no shape to make it . . . I can make it . . .

—Thanks, yeah . . . but you better get to the store . . .

She waved a hand dismissively.

—He, can, *wait*, she said, spacing her words to give them emphasis. He can wait. Here . . .

She handed Gary the diver's belt and helped him into the backpack.

—What you got in here, sack of cement?

Gary laughed. No fair peeking.

—What movie's that from? said Gretchen, rinsing out the mugs. No fair peeking? The way you said it, too. Are these anchovies?

—Movie? I haven't been to the movies since, since *King Kong*.

—What, the original?

—Yeah, I guess . . . Lloyd Bridges . . . terrible movie, incidentally.

Gretchen stopped doing stuff with coffee mugs, sighed and shook her head.

—Something crazy's happening here and I'm scrubbing out

mugs. And we're discussing movies. And it was Jeff Bridges, and that was the remake.

She turned and looked at Gary sitting awkwardly at the little kitchen table. He was folding up a pizza carton and looked both pathetic and hopeful at the same time, like she was going to sort everything out for him. Make it all right again.

—What are you going to do, Gary?

He shrugged. Go on *Oprah*, maybe? Weight loss is a big thing on her show.

—Seriously. I don't know if I can help. What can I do?

Gary gestured helplessly with his hands. Do? What can anyone . . . ? Wait up . . . yeah, here we go . . .

He shouldered out of the backpack and unclipped the belt, standing up quickly.

—Look. Perfectly okay.

His hands went to his face. Sure feels weird. Has my face changed?

Gretchen put her head on one side, holding her hair back. Uh huh. You look real tired.

—I ache all over. Everything's hanging, sagging.

He moved his head in stiff circles, stretching his arms.

—Maybe it's over, said Gretchen.

Gary shook his head, loosening his neck. I thought that before. It comes and goes. Jesus, I am tired.

He fell into a chair, rubbing his face.

—You should maybe see a doctor?

Gary laughed bleakly. For what? A real heavy pill, maybe? Strap me to a hospital bed for five thousand bucks a week? I don't think I'm insured for this.

He cocked his head, listening. Is that who I think it is?

Gretchen had heard it too, while Gary had been speaking. The familiar wavery whine of Vandergelder calling her name. All the way across the yard, around the houses.

—He can see his car in the drive still, she said.

59

—Gretchen, I gotta ask. Vandergelder. That fuck. Why? You could do better.

Gretchen raised her eyebrows a little. Well, thank you.

—None of my business, I guess.

—Well, I thought we were talking about your problem. We're pretty casual about it all of a sudden. Listen, I better get the groceries. I need to think about this. Can I get you anything? Maybe you better stay in for a bit. I mean, of course you better stay in. This is ridiculous. I'll try to think of something.

Gary thanked her, and she added the stuff he'd need to a neat list she'd folded into her jeans pocket. Bunch of TV dinners, beer, Surf-n-Snacks, Oreo cookies, basic foodstuffs.

—I can't believe we're being so calm about this, said Gretchen, like it was bursitis or something.

—Yeah, but believe me, I don't feel too peaceful about it. Scared shitless is how I feel about it. No, helpless. Like a baby.

—Maybe if you can work out how it happened we can sort of undo it. It's hard to think about right now.

—Yeah, but, our secret, right?

—Oh? I thought I'd stand in the mall fountain and hand out flyers.

They heard Vandergelder again.

—I better go. I'll look by later. Take care.

Gary called after her. Hey, Gretchen?

Gretchen turned in the hall.

—We'll get married when you get back with the beers. Bring a preacher.

She let herself out. Gary grinned. He felt good about telling her. She hadn't screamed and run into the street. She'd been cool and clear about it, as much as you could be. And she was buying his groceries. Then he felt the edge of the table graze down his shin.

FOUR

Miracle Jesus Salami

Gary grabbed the first thing he could, the skillet, but it wasn't enough to stop him rising to the ceiling. With his boots pulling his legs down and the skillet in his hand, the first part of him to hit the ceiling was his butt. He hung there, like his belt was on a hook, and wondered what to do. If he dropped the pan he could twist around and push himself down, maybe grab the table, reach the backpack. He heard a voice through the window.

—And what the heck are you playing at, neighbor?

Gary twisted his head up to see Vandergelder standing at the open kitchen window. The twinkly blue eyes and shiny cheeks, the weird knit shirt. Gary closed his eyes, prayed for him to go a long way away and die.

—Hello? I'm talking to you.

Gary opened his eyes. He had to say something. Put him on the defensive.

—You're feeling better today? Fit enough to take a crawl through the shrubbery to kiss your pension goodbye?

—Don't be so unpleasant. Is Gretchen in there? And what in the good Lord's name are you doing up there?

—Gretchen, said Gary thoughtfully, as if the name rang a distant bell in his head, Yeah, she was here. She's gone to get your goddamn groceries. If you weren't skulking around people's backyards you'd have seen her leave.

Vandergelder stood rubbing his chin a while.

—So what on earth are you doing up there on the ceiling?

61

Gary sighed. Did it matter what he said?

—I've suddenly become weightless and I'm flying around like an astronaut. No, I was making a pancake in this skillet here and tossed myself instead. Not that it's any of your business, incidentally, but it's actually good for my back. Gretchen hooks me up here from time to time when it gets bad. Only room in the house with a steel in the ceiling. You never knew we had something going together, did you? Sometimes she walks up and down my spine in stilettos, that's good for it too.

Vandergelder smiled. Well, neighbor, you're going to be up there a while because I need her to look after me. Full time.

—Don't you have some skin to shed or something? Gary asked reasonably.

—Oh dear. A chip off the old block, Vandergelder said, shaking his head.

Gary waved the skillet. Mi casa su casa.

Vandergelder squeezed back through the fence, making sure his shirt didn't get caught, and disappeared, whistling. Gary dropped the skillet, tucked his knees under his chest and rocked backward, pushing the ceiling as he straightened his legs. He dove down to the floor and looped an arm through the backpack strap, wrestling himself into a sitting position while he buckled it on. Priority one, he told himself: get the blinds pulled all over the house. This is not Sea World, busloads of tourists flattening their pasty faces against the glass. He swayed around the house like a mall wino, closing the drapes, thinking through the connection between swimming and weightlessness.

—Should be able to attain some kind of equilibrium if I get the weights right, fly around the place like a big aquarium.

In the hall, where the walls were closest, he took off the backpack and the boots and experimented with the diver's belt, unclipping the plastic-skinned lead slugs until he could just hang there like a watch part in one of those acrylic paperweights. He practiced a few simple turns and rolls, always trying to finish what he thought of as the right way up so he could orientate himself. He adopted extravagant poses, just for the hell of it, doing a Superman, and a Bruce Lee, and a John Travolta. But there were unforeseen complications. If he wasn't anchored to something, he was always moving. It seemed impossible not to be turning one way or the other, and every effort to counteract one movement just led to another.

He tentatively punted into the living room, pulling himself around by the furniture. There was, he discovered, no such thing as up and down, no internal compass to balance him, not even the sensation of blood rushing to his head to tell him he was upside-down. Up and down only made sense visually, and it was surprisingly easy for this model to stop functioning; sometimes the whole room just looked upside-down, or tipped on its side, instead of him. He found he could spin the whole house around without the furniture crashing down on his head.

There were other novel effects; in this house-upside-down mode he could let things he'd picked up float up to the floor, something he found stupidly amusing, scoring points for getting magazines to stick to the table. For the first time he actually felt exhilarated. He knew he'd take a fall when the effect wore off but it was worth it. He was grinning like a kid. He pushed from wall to wall around the house with growing confidence, keeping the place upside down out of preference, as it seemed like exploring a drowned, sunken world. Automatically he found himself doing a kind of breaststroke which was strangely reassuring, but didn't actually make him go any further. After a bit more experimentation, he found he could spin by just tucking into a roll, and slow the rotation by stretching out again, but it seemed impossible to control direction and speed once he'd made the initial push from a surface, and he longed to be able to fly in a controlled curve. Once there was a moment of thrashing panic when he thought he'd come to a stop in the middle of the room, but after a few tense seconds he drifted within reach of a speaker cabinet and anchored himself to it gratefully.

The doorbell sounded, so he used the speaker cable to get to the shelf unit and crawled along that to where he could reach the door and look around it. The doorbell went again. A pale face pressed up against the small frosted pane, and he heard a voice.

—Gary? You okay? It's Gretchen.

He chimneyed up along the hall, the doorway directly overhead, and turned the latch, trying to get the house into its right-way-up mode for the visitor, as he didn't want her falling into the kitchen. Gretchen pushed the door open and knocked him into a spin back down the hall. She slammed the door shut behind her and dropped the grocery sack.

—Oh my God . . .

Gary managed to get a grip on the kitchen door, but not before smacking the back of his head on the frame.

—Shit.

Gretchen helped steady him and get him upright next to the stove.

—So, he said woozily, the store busy? You get the Cheerios?

—Gary, she said, we have to talk.

He rubbed his head, getting the world the right way up again.

—Yeah, but you better get back, your old man was here and he's pissed.

—What, he was here in his chair? He's *not* my old man.

—Miracle cure, apparently. Looked pretty shifty about it. But these are the days of miracles and shit, like Ray's Jesus salami.

—What are you talking about? said Gretchen from the hall where she was picking up the groceries.

—My pal Ray had some salami with Jesus' face in it. I'm sorry now that I treated it like a joke.

—What? she said, unloading the groceries on the kitchen table.

64

—I ate it.

—Gary, really, we have to sort something out for you here.

—Vandergelder . . .

—I parked up the street. He can't see your front door, can he?

—Unless his eyes come out on stalks. Which we mustn't dismiss out of hand.

Gretchen bared her teeth and threatened Gary with a loaf of bread, the type with a crust that you had to cut, that he hadn't ordered.

—Listen, will you, and stop the stupid jokes? What you've got is maybe real important, this is like a miracle or something, whatever you think. I've been thinking about this, and it's really a miracle. What else is it?

Gary groaned, and shook his head.

—I am really so disappointed, Gretchen. Do you really believe that? Do you really believe what you just said? *Maybe* it's a miracle, but so was Ray's salami. Calling it a fucki – he caught a look from Gretchen – calling it a miracle doesn't help. I don't need the place crawling with nuns, crutches all over the porch. What's miracle got to do with it? This is me, Gary Wilder, your kindly neighbor. I make a few hundred bucks in a month, that's a miracle. I haven't been to church since, since I got married, and that doesn't count. That was a drive-thru. You can't believe that shit, Gretchen, tell me you can't. I need some help here, not somebody touching the hem of my garment. Miracles don't look good on me. I don't *do* miracles.

Gretchen had been listening to all this with her face down, the stray strand of hair catching the light from the crack between the blinds.

—I don't mean like a Bible miracle, she said so quietly Gary had to strain to hear her. I mean like some kind of natural miracle, like a discovery, like discovering fire.

She gestured with the bread, searching for the right words.

65

—I mean it's something that can maybe really benefit the world. I mean, you don't feel sick or anything? Right, and you haven't been breathing any, like, gases, pollution or drugs?

Gary couldn't help but give a little laugh.

—Right, so it's just happened, at random, so it could maybe happen to someone else . . .

Gary realized she was skirting around something, afraid of sounding stupid maybe. He nodded for her to go on.

—It could be like the next step, she said. The next step in evolution, like we were all fishes? And we crawled out, and learned to walk?

Gary thought about this. I don't know. Shouldn't I have sprouted wings from my shoulderblades? Shouldn't we all, if it's evolutionary? If you're talking about flying like a bird? And little by little, maybe just get some little downy duckling feathers for a few thousand years first. Also, I can't believe it's that important, on that scale. No one else is affected. This is just me, not the star child at the end of two thousand close encounters, whatever. I mean I don't feel evolved, just a little queasy. I wish I was back to normal, I really do.

Gary wondered if this was true even as he said it.

—Do we know it's only you? Maybe you're not the only one. Somewhere on the other side of the world maybe the same thing is happening. Maybe a little Chinese girl is floating around a temple someplace and being worshipped. Not everything gets on CNN.

She watched him bobbing up and down in the doorway like a fishing float.

—Lasted a long time this time, huh?

—Since you left.

—You have to face it, Gary, you may never get back to normal. Maybe this *is* normal. You have to deal with it.

—More *National Enquirer* than CNN, wouldn't you say?

They were both quiet.

66

—I better get back, she said eventually.

—Can you please come back? I mean, you're the only one who knows. I don't want to tell anyone else yet. We need to work out how we're going to do that, if we have to, if the effect doesn't go . . .

—You know that Lone Ranger joke? What do you mean *we*, white man? I kind of wish you'd never told me, Gary, I got enough to worry about at the moment.

—So you'll come back?

Gretchen was fooling with her keys, looking at her watch.

—I guess I have to. He gets to sleep around midnight. I'll come by then. Leave your kitchen door open. But please, just don't say, hey, Gretchen, thanks, on my way out. Please. You want your backpack on?

Gary thought he'd better weight down for a bit, get himself something to eat, whatever, and together they buckled it up around his waist, her hair brushing his face. When she was at the front door Gary said, Hey, Gretchen, thanks. On your way out.

Gretchen rolled her eyes and left. He grinned.

—Thought the girl had gotten religion there for a moment, actually a dangerous response and one we must anticipate. Jesus flakes tearing their shirts on the lawn, me on the roof with the Pope. She might have been some kind of Christian too, name like Gretchen, didn't think of that possibility, have to be careful. Those guys who don't wear zippers or have iceboxes have names like Gretchen, terrible names. Ray's salami, should never have eaten it. I'm sorry, Jesus, please can I have my weight back, well, like ninety percent would be fine, you could keep the stuff from around my belly, make up for the salami, with interest . . .

He put a TV dinner in the microwave, and his head in his hands.

—I don't want to be a miracle, Jesus, he said in a tiny little

67

voice that sounded pathetic even to him, feeling his eyes get hot and itchy. Please make me ordinary again.

He stared bleakly at the little glowing shrine, watching his Mister Hunk-o-Cod BatterBrunch revolve in the golden light, until the timer bell pinged.

FIVE

Gary's Air Salute

Gary picked up the phone.

—Gary? Gretchen.

—Hi, yeah, hang on . . .

—Gary? You there?

—Uh huh. Just settling down. Woof. I feel like I've been hit by a small truckload of gym equipment. Jesus, it's so heavy. I should check the scales. You sung your old man to sleep, all tucked up in his jammies? I bet they got a drop seat.

—It's eight o'clock, Gary. A little early even for an invalid. Listen, I don't think I can come by later, but I've been thinking about getting help. I think you're right about doctors. They'd treat you like a lab rat.

—So who wouldn't, apart from nuns?

—Listen. NASA. The moonshot guys. Think about it. Those guys know about weightlessness. They could be sympathetic. They'd certainly be interested, they wouldn't charge your account. They may be able to help. Maybe they have a special weightless room or something. I think I read about it. What do you think?

—Um. Kinda makes sense, I guess. I don't know. They're linked to the military? I don't want to talk to any soldiers about this. They'll get me flapping my arms over Libya with a fucking Nikon up my ass.

—How are you now?

—Weight? Normal, I guess. I feel tired. I ache, and I got

69

bruises all over. I mean, I know it's happened, but it seems so stupid when I think about it. I'd hate to get some rocket scientists over here to put an oxygen tent over the house and I'd just be some slob in shorts drinking beer. How impressed are they going to be? I can't predict this. Hey, wait a minute . . . this is weird, now *this* is weird . . .

—What? Gary? What's happening?

—I wish you could see this . . . actually, it's just my arm waving about, I mean I guess you can visualize that, it's not very exciting . . . except that it's the effect, just my arm, though, I'm watching it . . .

—You mean just your arm is weightless?

—Uh huh. Just my left arm. I can bend it, move it, but when I . . . weird. And now my arm is down, and it feels . . . like something is kind of playing with me, the effect is going through me in, little waves . . . kind of sensual actually . . .

—Wow. So. Anyway. NASA. What do you think?

—I'm not sure. What would I do, phone them up and say, Hi, I'm doing a moonwalk in my living room, can I have a silver suit and some freeze-dried kelp tablets?

—I thought about that, too.

—Kelp tablets?

—You have a camcorder?

—A VCR?

—No, the movie camera you plug into the VCR.

—I don't even have a VCR. I don't have a CD player. None of that initials shit. Except a TV, of course, but that's more like a word . . . Hey, now my foot's got it, my left foot . . .

—Okay. We get a camcorder, and I shoot a movie of you doing your stuff, and we send the cassette to NASA, and we say how they can contact us. No address, maybe we ask them to run an ad in the classifieds.

—Kind of secret-agent set-up.

—You got it. We control the meeting. We make the conditions.

70

—I want a shoe phone.

—Huh?

—Maxwell . . .

—Oh hey, there he goes . . . the big baby . . . Can you hear him? I'll get a camera tomorrow at the mall, you can pay me later, I'll sneak it round. *Okay*, Mr Vandergelder, I'm coming . . . later, Gary . . .

—Later.

Gary started feeling better about the whole deal. He squeezed the remote, thumbing the buttons extra hard to compensate for the fading batteries, and shuffled through the channels like a deck of bright cards. He liked the sound of this NASA thing, if they could keep the military out of it. He felt vaguely good about NASA. He remembered the gorgeous colors of the images from the moon-landing, a reflection of Old Glory in a glittering black visor. Serious shirtsleeves in the control room, concerned faces underlit by monitors. And they had hair like his. These guys could help. Gretchen was a genius. Yippee.

He used his returned weight, wondering briefly where it had been, maybe on vacation to Gravity World, to do some important stuff round the house, like drinking a beer while he took a dump. Walking around the house with all the drapes pulled waiting for something weird to happen had a pleasantly nostalgic sixties feel to it, now he came to think of it. He rippled through the sagging pile of albums behind the couch and put *The Inner Mystique* on the deck to enhance the mood, the side with the long instrumentals. Occasionally he'd feel the effect come and go in an arm or a leg, and he began to think that maybe it really was wearing off. He was surprised to realize he didn't want it to. Almost. Maybe. He was on his fourth beer when the telephone rang again. It was Paul French in LA. Gary was a little slow getting up to speed on the subject of the no-caster. It seemed like weeks ago. Then Paul mentioned a sum of money that woke him up with a snap, said he wanted the guitar tomorrow, could Gary deliver.

—It's a little difficult, Paul. I'm laid up with this viral thing, hit me real sudden. I'm not in the shop all week.

—What is this shit? I got Shaney Michaelson, from Hairsbreadth? He's practically messing in his pocket over this. It's as much as I could do, promise him tomorrow. They've got a major coast-to-coast starting Saturday and he's gonna care about your viral thing?

Shaney Michaelson, thought Gary blankly. Never heard of the fuck. Paul always liked to talk like an LA big shot, dramatizing every ordinary transaction. It made Gary tired.

—I'll get Carl to open up the store, Paul. Stop being a big fucking girl's pantyliner. But you're going to have to get over here, we're not a delivery service, and I want cash, he won't take anything else so don't fuck around. We got a deal?

—Viral thing, huh? You been taking it in the ass again? Losing weight? Hair falling out?

Gary's heart sank. Did he have AIDS? Weird things happened to guys with AIDS.

—Pleasure doing business with you, Paul. And tell your wife thanks, it was as great as always. The ice cubes were a nice touch.

—Wither and die, Gar. Viral thing, yeah, right. Ha ha.

—Cash money. He'll be there in the a.m.

Gary phoned Carl and left a message with his mom for him to stop by and pick up the keys and some instructions from the mail box. She sounded distracted, and kept breaking off to tell the little girl something, so he repeated it was really important and there'd be some kind of bonus for Carl. Then he weighed himself on the scales in the bathroom.

—Back to my normal healthy weight, which is necessarily slightly overweight for someone of my build. Marcie always on my case, join the gym, fuck about with some weights, me in a fucking leotard, I really do think not. Fag jock shit.

To pass the time he made himself a fat peanut butter sandwich on the grainy brown bread, tearing the crusts off, and sat in front of the television. He was pretty convinced it was over, whatever it had been. Or he was trying to convince himself that it was, he couldn't tell. He wrote Carl his instructions, telling him to deposit the money in the Wilder Sounds account. He dropped the shop keys in an envelope and ran his tongue along the sour gum edge.

—If I'm back to normal in the morning I'll go in myself. I'll probably be back to normal.

He opened the front door and gazed around. The mailbox was nailed to the front of the house where it was less of a temptation to the slouching slackers from across the street who had knocked it off its pole. He didn't like leaving the keys in it anyway, but it was too late to change plans. He tucked the envelope under a yellowing mall flyer, pausing to read it.

—Men's leisure suits fifty-nine ninety-five and built in Russia I bet, fucking Soviet cardboard laundry.

He carefully lowered the tin lid so it wouldn't squeak, realizing he was doing everything in secret all of a sudden. The night air smelled good, and the stars were out. He scanned the sky like an Indian brave, in tune with the elemental forces of nature, looking for the constellations he'd learned as a kid, intoning them to himself in a Boy's World of Science way.

—The Big Dipper. Orion the Hunter. Zorba the Greek. Beppo the Clown. Cancer the . . . disease? Like Alzheimer's. Like AIDS. Paul French, the asshole.

It only needed Tinkerbell to trace a sparkly twirl in the sky to enhance the atmosphere of childlike wonder. From a few miles away he heard some thin pops that could have been backfire or cherry bombs but he knew to be gunfire, and distant dogs jerked from their twitchy sleep to bark at the night. Gary went back inside and slid the bolts.

SIX

Anchovies

Next morning, around ten, Kent Treacy limped up Gary's driveway and rang the bell. His feet were blistering in his Z-Mart shoes and his shirt was outside his pants and he was hot and very tired. He had walked a long way.

—Hey, far out, he thought. This is the place. Just like when we used to pick him up in the truck. Folks all gone now. C'mon, answer the door, man. Everything shut up and daaaaaark.

He peered through the frosted pane in the door, cupped his hands round his mouth.

—Gary, he said, it's me, Kent. Can I get a glass of water?

Inside, nothing moved, everything was quiet. There'd been nobody at the store, either, when he'd loped past earlier. He went round the side of the house and lifted himself up to the high slot window in the garage wall.

—Pickup's here, he grunted, scraping his knees as he dropped back down. He went around to the back, rattled the kitchen door.

—Gar? It's Kent, man . . .

After a minute or so the door opened a little way and a blond woman looked out at him without saying anything.

—Hi. Is Gary here? I need to tell him something and I need a glass of water. Are you his wife?

From inside he heard Gary's voice say, It's okay, let the guy in. He sounded none too keen about it, though. The blonde opened the door a little further, all the time looking around as if

74

there were Vietcong in the bushes. As soon as he squeezed in she shut the door.

—Wait here, she said. Help yourself to a glass of water. She went into the hallway and shut the door behind her. He heard voices.

—Gary? he said. He went to the sink and ran the faucet into his mouth, then turned it off and stared into the sink. Gary, are these anchovies?

The door opened and the blond woman came back in. You're eating those? she said, in a tone of disgusted disbelief.

Kent shrugged. I'm real hungry. Where's Gary?

—He's okay, give him a couple minutes. I'm Gretchen.

Kent looked blank.

—I live next door? she added, in a hello-in-there voice. Kent sat on the floor and began unlacing his shoes, picking at the tangled knots. Gretchen noticed his skinned knuckles and broken nails.

—I wore these for the funeral, he said. Normally, I don't like to wear them although on occasion, of course, but today I . . .

His voice trailed off. The door opened and Gary came in, looking somehow guilty, or drunk, or both. Gretchen watched him hold the furniture. Kent snapped a lace, swore, talked without looking up.

—Gary, I gotta tell you what I saw in the desert, man, lights in the sky and . . .

Gary signed for a time-out.

—Kent, please, right now I got other things on my mind. Things have happened . . .

Gretchen looked at him wide-eyed, mouthing the word no, shaking her head. Kent saw her.

—Sure, man, you got something going here, that's okay. Do your thing, I'm cool.

—Something going? I don't think you know what's happening here, Kent, you really wouldn't understand.

Kent gave up with the knots and kicked his shoes off.

—Oh, wow, that feels good . . . whatever, man. Uh, can I crash here tonight? I think I lost my car . . .

Gary breathed heavily through his nose, nodding his head.

—You think you lost your car . . . okay, I'll buy that. But let me give you a ride to your folks' place, huh? It's a bit inconvenient right now for you to stay.

Kent stood up and peeled another anchovy from the sink, humming. Gary suddenly saw how thin the guy was.

—Kent, are you hungry?

—I've been walking, Gar, and I've been right out there in the desert, man . . . the lights . . .

—Yeah, the lights. Right. Can I build you a sandwich? Peanut butter? I could sure use a beer too, as well also. Gretchen? Wanna join us?

—Go right ahead without me. So, Kent, you're an old friend of Gary's, huh? Live round here?

Kent was balancing on one leg, hooking a sock off. His foot was red raw.

—Look, this is what shoes do to your feet, man, leather caskets, your feet can't breathe all tied up in boxes . . .

—Talking of breathing, said Gretchen, can I ask you to put your shoes and socks outside?

Gary chuckled as he took the beers from the icebox. Kent opened the door and arranged his footwear neatly on the step.

—Gary, she said, do you want me to give Kent a ride home?

He twisted the cap off a beer and handed it to Kent. That okay?

Kent took the beer and drained it noisily down his throat. Beautiful, he said, and belched.

—No, Kent, is it okay if we give you a ride home? Like I said, it's a little inconvenient right now to have you to stay.

—Sure, Gar, whatever. Inconvenient. Weird word.

76

Gretchen leaned toward Gary, pushing her hands into her jean pockets.

—Gary? Can we talk?

He watched Kent craning his neck to look into the sink. He'd stuck his thumb in the empty bottle neck and was swinging it like a pendulum.

—Excuse us a second, Kent?

Kent hummed to himself. Gary and Gretchen went through the hall into the living room, closing the doors behind them. On the coffee table was the silver Panasonic camcorder she'd bought at the mall, like a big mean robot war insect in a nest of styrofoam packaging.

—Listen, Gary, we do not need this. *I* do not need this. My life is quite rich enough right now without Captain Trips out there eating anchovies out of the sink and mumbling about lights in the sky. I simply cannot deal with him as well as you. As well as *Mister* Vandergelder. You want to include him, fine, but include me out, right? I have passed my quota of helpless men to go shopping for. There you go.

Gary sat on the couch, looking bleak.

—Gretchen, what can I do? I'm dropping hints heavy enough to crack ice in Alaska. I can't physically kick the guy out because he's a complication. He's a friend, a buddy. You want a life free of complications, write poetry in Vermont and wear a big fucking flowery hat.

—Don't get snitty with me, Gary. Just understand that we had some kind of plan, and that's fine, but it doesn't include mysterious friends turning up out of the past and eating anchovies out the sink.

—It's jake with me, Gretchen. I hate the things. Let him finish the fucking anchovies and I'll drive him home and the whole thing's over anyway and no harm done, except I'm out four hundred bucks for a camera. I've been waiting all night and

77

all that's happened is these funny little ripples or waves going through me. Like it's wearing out. Showtime's over. The stripy tape's coming down and we got to give the tickets back.

They looked at each other.

—He was a good friend of yours?

—Oh, sure. The best. Here, I have a photo somewhere . . .

He squatted down at the cupboard under the TV and started pulling a whole load of papers and stuff onto the floor. Gretchen picked up a tattered old *Rolling Stone*.

—Nineteen sixty-*nine*? You really believe in keeping in touch, right?

—And I'd be buying it still if I wanted to keep in touch with developments in male grooming and footwear for assholes. But no, it's not like I collect this shit, I just still have it. You accumulate all kinds of shit. Jesus, look at this. I don't know why. Yeah, here we are . . .

It was a yellowing clipping from the Newdale *News*, Buddy Leonard's Hits 'n' Clicks Page, with a four-column halftone of The High above a gushing blurb promising a bright future for the Newdale combo. Printed immediately after they split up for good.

—This is you?

Gary watched her smiling in that patronizing yet kind of irritatingly loving way some women do when looking at photographs of guys doing guy's stuff, like you were cute little boys.

—Second from right. Kent in centre.

—Oh, look at this . . . your hair! Hey, he's cute. That's really the same guy?

—Yeah. But what about me? Am I cute? It was my group. I get to be cute if it's my group.

Gretchen put her head on one side and pouted.

—Okay, you're cute too. Especially your stripy jeans. And the big hipster belt there . . . oh my *God*!

She was giggling. Her face really changed when she laughed.

78

Gary acted grumpy and stuffed the papers back in the cupboard, pushing them back in there any old way.

—Kids today, he said, no respect for their elders.

—Just how old do you think I am, Gary?

He was old enough to know there was no way he was playing that one.

—Yeah. Maybe Kent's finished the anchovies. Wanna see?

—Not really. But I guess we should look in on him. You shouldn't drive him home, just in case. He can get a cab. Anyway, I have to sneak back around the corner. My employer will be calling the cops by now.

—Jesus, Gretchen . . .

—A joke. He's just a little, um, possessive.

It was Gary's turn to pout. They went back to the kitchen. It was empty. Gary looked in the sink.

—He's nothing if not thorough.

He called Kent's name, put his head out the door, looked around.

—I guess he's wandered off again. Kind of a theme with the guy. We get to keep his shoes, though.

—Yeah, well, talking of wandering off . . . I'll drop by later. My afternoon is free.

—Sure. If you see Kent arguing with a trashcan, tell him hi.

—You're worried about him?

—He'll be back. Twenty-four hours, twenty-four years. I don't think he knows the difference anymore, I really don't.

As she brushed past him in the doorway he felt her breast press against his arm. Gary went back into the living room, head full of disruptive thought patterns, and opened the drapes. He was tired of hiding in the dark. He sat on the couch and scowled at the camcorder's instruction book.

—What fucking language is this written in anyway? Why can't I read anymore? Who's responsible for this shit?

He kept thinking about the touch of Gretchen's breast, how

surprised he was by it for some reason. While he was on the subject he thought about Terry's breasts too.

—I have to call them. Her. I have to call her. Jesus. I stood the kid up, and she's beautiful. Tell her something she'll believe. Blacked out on the freeway, tubes up my nose, calling from the oxygen tent. He dialed the Buena Viva and she answered.

—Don't hang up, Terry, please don't hang . . .

She hung up. He redialed, got the busy tone, kept redialing until she answered.

—I'm sorry, Terry, I'm a total piece of shit and I'm sorry. Please don't hang up . . .

—I'm waiting.

—There's nothing I can tell you except I'm sorry and I couldn't reach you last night. Jesus, what a complete nightmare . . .

—That's it? I have another line coming in, if you'll excuse me, Mr Wilder.

She hung up. Gary grimaced, grinding his teeth, and beat the handset into the seat cushion again and again like he was clubbing it to death.

—Shitshitshitshitshitshitshitshit . . .

He was so angry at himself he failed to notice immediately when he rose slowly from the chair.

—Whoa . . .

He turned over and floated up toward the ceiling, hanging onto the handset like a lifeline. His butt hit the ceiling first, and he hung there, willing his heart to slow up.

—Uh, Gary . . .

He jerked his head around. Kent stood in the doorway, dressed in his shorts with the bottle still hanging from his thumb.

—I just woke up. Is that sandwich still a possibility?

SEVEN

Fusebox Stash Nostalgia Rush

Gary looked down at Kent looking up at him on the ceiling, and not for the first time tried to imagine the profile of his friend's event horizon. What kind of planet did he live on where the natural response to finding someone floating up to the ceiling was to ask for a sandwich?

—Could you fix it yourself? he said at length. I'm kind of busy right now.

—Okay, Kent said, going into the kitchen. You want one?

—Not right now, but thanks anyway.

Right now Gary wanted to close the drapes more than just about anything in the whole wide world. He felt horribly exposed, like being on the john with the door open. He reeled in the phone cable, very delicately, between his finger and thumb, following it down to the wall socket, and hid behind the couch, wedging himself against the wall.

—So this is where my Swiss Army knife got to.

He blew a cloud of dust off it and levered out a mysterious pointy thing with his thumbnail.

—And now I know what this thing's for, crafty Swiss bastards foreseeing the use of weightlessness gas in alpine warfare . . .

He held the knife in his fist, pointy thing sticking between his fingers, and stabbed the floor with it, anchoring himself to the carpet. He pulled himself out from behind the couch, along the wall, and stabbed the floor again. Kent came in chewing on something that looked like a burnt brick.

—You hate that carpet, huh, Gary, he said, peanut butter cleaving to his palate.

—Kent, you want to get the drapes for me? It's a little . . .

—Bright. Sure. I got it.

Kent closed the drapes and ate his sandwich while Gary spiraled casually around the room.

—So, what do you think? said Gary, unable to resist it any longer.

—Okay, but rye would be my bread of choice. Hey, I got places to go today. I gotta drop by the club, man.

Gary felt the elevator lurch in his stomach and propelled himself over the couch, just in time.

—You want to go where? he grunted, dropping gracelessly onto the cushions. He felt his body weight like a huge dark presence, like a stranger making room for himself inside, taking up occupancy, giving his internal organs a good kicking. It was uncomfortable, reassuring, oddly disappointing, and tiring, all at once.

—My stash may still be in the fusebox, said Kent.

—At the club? Klub 45? I don't think so.

—I have to check it out.

Gary scratched his head. He felt like getting out of the house, for sure. This was like being sick, an invalid.

—Okay, he said. But I'll need my diver's weights and shit, just in case, you know . . .

—It's flooded, said Kent.

Gary parked in the delivery bay, carefully and stupidly leaving the weights and the backpack on the seat where he could easily grab them in any in-cab emergency situation, and they walked back around onto Main, stood on the sidewalk outside Ed's Bait Shoppe, sheltering their eyes with their hands. Gary pointed up.

—You can see the bolt stubs for the old sign, see?

—I can smell the surf, said Kent.

—I can hear the grass grow.

—I can see for miles.

—I can . . . Tina Turner.

—I can Eleanor Roosevelt.

Gary snorked. Eleanor *Roosevelt?*

Kent shrugged. So who can remember who Eisenhower's wife was?

—Mamie, said Gary authoritatively.

—Mamie Van fucking *Doren.*

Gary looked at Kent. You telling me Eisenhower was married to Mamie Van fucking Doren?

—Of the New Hampshire Van fucking Dorens.

They stood nodding reasonably for a while.

—You want to go inside? asked Gary eventually.

—We have to set up the gig, man . . .

—Listen, if I grab hold of you suddenly . . .

Kent held up his big finny hands. Whoa . . . I like you, Gar, but not in that way . . .

—If I grab you, right, it's because the thing's happening, and we have to leave . . .

—Do your thing, man.

—But listen, Kent, this is real important, so please pay attention FOR FUCK'S SAKE . . . I don't *want* to do my thing in Ed's Bait Shoppe, okay? So if it starts, you grab me and don't let go, and we split, and I do my thing at home.

—Everything's cool.

They went inside. It smelled moist and mealy in there, pretty much like it smelled when it had been a nightclub, Gary reflected. Ed stood behind the counter, fumbling with some clear plastic boxes. He looked up and smiled.

—Mr Gary Wilder. What can I do for you gentlemen?

—Hello, Ed. I need a box of knots for my line. Ha ha. No, actually I'm here with an old friend of mine . . . Kent?

Kent was staring straight up at a point on the ceiling, in a kind of petrified praying mantis pose.

—Well, moving right along now, continued Gary, we used to play here back in the dark ages. Same band. When it was a club?

—You don't say, Gary? This place used to be a club? He whistled through his teeth. You should tell us all the story one night at the Your Favorite. The guys'd love that. Musician, you say. Sure, go ahead, poke around, bring back the old days. There's a whole bunch of old stuff in a closet upstairs, posters, box of tapes, photos, I haven't looked at for years.

Gary's eyes widened. Tapes? You're kidding, right?

—Of course I'm kidding. You try running a bait shop. But go on up and take a look, you and your musician friend.

—Thanks, said Gary. Someday you'll get to come back here when it's a kiddy-porn store and bore some evil-eyed slope about when it used to be a bait shop. Kent? Hello?

—The fusebox is upstairs.

—What he say?

—He'd like a look upstairs?

The door opened and Ed moved Gary aside.

—Excuse me, gentlemen. Paying customer.

Gary and Kent climbed the concrete stair to the first floor where the 'ballroom' had been, now just a boxroom. Gary felt suddenly fake somehow. None of this meant anything to him. Nothing was making contact. He wasn't getting any kind of nostalgia buzz. It was a bait shop.

—Wow, said Kent. Boxes.

They mooched around a bit, kicking boxes.

—Look at this, said Kent, peeling back a corner of dirty orange wallpaper. They still got the same wallpaper. Awesome. And the stage . . . look, Gar, this is where I trashed that sunburst Framus . . .

He ran his fingertips over a dent in the metal edging to the little raised stage area.

—This is ideal, Gar . . .

Gary frowned at him, sitting on the edge of the stage, his crazy face all lit up.

—Sure, Kent. It's ideal. Right.

He gazed around the place vacantly. If he tried, he could summon up memories of playing here, but they seemed second-hand. Used memories. Like a bunch of daytime TV actors in the cheap fiberboard set of his life. Kent's voice came from over in the corner. He was standing on a chair, his head in the fusebox.

—My stash, man. Far out. This is like a sign. Let's go on the roof.

He jumped down, holding something small and silver, and grinning.

—I don't think this is a good idea, began Gary, but Kent was already swerving between boxes, heading for the door. Gary sighed and followed him, climbing the rungs set in the wall up to the hatch in the roof. This is not a good idea, he said to himself, but right at this moment I do not have a better one. I do not have a single idea in my goddamn head. Except this big fucking dumb one, so I guess it wins. He struggled up out onto the roof, feeling a big kahuna wave of heat whomp back off the sticky bitumen. He squinted painfully in the light. Kent was sitting on the edge, looking out over Main to Bernie's Bargain Hut, through the tangle of pylons beyond to the disused cement works. Gary joined him, gripping the edge of the roof, feeling the hot sticky tar bite into his palms. Kent was rolling the little silver foil ball between his fingertips. A soundtrack of cars and conversations blurred up from the street. Way overhead, a plane crackled like summer thunder, a silver needle ripping a frayed white thread through the blue.

—Newdale is so beautiful, man, I'd forgotten, said Kent quietly.

—Mm. Me too, said Gary. In fact, even now, with it spread out before us, I find it hard to remember how beautiful it is.

—Yeah, *right*, said Kent, and hummed a tune it took Gary a while to remember.

—'Shady Tree Party'?

Kent nodded, and Gary sang the chorus, about as far out of key as you can get without actually quite coming back in the other side.

—Summer's hummin', it's the time to be free, something something . . . under a shady tree . . .

—We're all comin', said Kent.

—We sang that? We're all coming?

They snickered.

—This is ideal, said Kent. Just like we used to in the old days. Same guys. Same roof. Same drugs. Ideal.

—Hello? Hey, Kent, walk a mile in the coffee. Wake up and smell my shoes. Things are a little unusual for me right now. Not exactly ideal. You may have noticed.

—We'd need to find a place for the boxes.

Gary tried hard not to get involved in any way with Kent's thing about boxes. Especially right at this moment.

—Kent, look at me, listen. I'm floating about sometimes. You saw me. This is not strictly usual, yes? For me, I guess, anyway.

Kent looked at him, and his eyes, for the first time, looked as if they were hooked up to a nervous system somewhere within our own solar system.

—Usual, he said. Weird word. You-zew-al. Oozhval. Ussue-el. Yush-well. No, Gar, it's real obvious. Usual has nothing to do with it. The world has lost its attraction for you.

Gary felt a slight tingling sensation, a little vascular excitement, and caught his breath.

—Actually, Kent, it's all starting to happen again. Just hold me, will you, I don't want to let go here, just grab my belt, I . . . oh fuck, don't let go . . .

Without changing his position at all, Gary knew he'd become weightless, and it had been super-quick this time, his body weight just vaporized in the sudden rush. Kent was holding his belt, and he was gripping onto the parapet, so there was really no danger of flying off, but this was the scariest yet, with no safety-net ceiling over his head.

—I have an idea, said Kent.

—You want to do a rooftop gig, like the Beatles, gasped Gary, nodding. Good, this is good.

—Come on, man, let's go. There's a thrill up on the hill.

Kent stood up, moved away from the edge, pulling Gary with him.

—Let *go*, man.

Gary's palms were studded with tiny sticky black diamonds. He swayed over backward, his feet in the air. Kent just pulled him along behind him to where the fire escape led over the parapet, down to the delivery bay in back of the store.

—Okay, Gar, grab it, you got it. I'm under you, man, I got your ankle here, you ain't going anywhere but down, you got it.

—What if somebody sees us? whined Gary, pushing up on the handrails, hooking his toes under the steps. The similarity to pulling himself underwater by the swimming pool ladder was so great he found himself holding his breath.

—What's to see? said Kent, hanging off the last step and dropping to the ground. There was nobody around anyway, and the pickup was right there. Gary got to the bottom step and pushed up until Kent could grab his ankle. Kent was guiding him up into the cab of the pickup when Ed came out the back door, looking at them warily.

—You guys get what you came for?

—Thanks, Ed, said Gary, pulling the safetybelt across his chest. But I got to fly . . .

—Yes indeed, said Kent, getting behind the wheel.

—Musicians, Ed spat, as the drive wheels spun on the pickup and it took off in a cloud of denture-coating white dust.

*

Gary winced as Kent crunched the gears yet again and swerved off-road, bouncing over a rutted vacant lot toward some dilapidated industrial units on the edge of town. Some of them were half demolished, and a couple of big dozers stood waiting for someone to show up. It was deserted and exactly like a set for a post-holocaust movie, right down to the busted Safeway cart with doll parts in it.

—We're here, man. Treaco. My old man's contribution to the march of global capitalism. Died a year before he did.

He braked in an extravagant skid, just kissing the corner of the building with the rear nerf bar.

—Jesus, Kent, said Gary, taking his arms down from bracing himself against the roof. You certainly haven't spent the last twenty-five years fine-tuning your driving skills, that's for sure.

—It don't matter when you don't have a license. You can drive how you want. It's the law. Come on, man.

Kent got out of the cab and kicked a buckled metal door open.

—Great security, said Gary, trying to stay upright as he followed him inside, weighed down by the backpack and the scuba belt. Inside was nothing but a big, big empty space filled with sunlight and cement dust.

—This was the warehouse, said Kent, searching amongst some bits of raggedy wood leaning against the wall. Dad kept all his boxes here, big boxes, they moved 'em all out . . .

—Ah, Kent . . . may I ask why we're here?

Kent didn't answer for a while, too busy looking for something.

—Here we go, he said, holding up two bits of thin flexible board, flapping them in the air. Bird wings.

—Okay, said Gary in quiet admiration. All right . . . I get it.

Kent passed him the boards and he held one in each hand, out at arm's length, while Kent took off the scuba belt and unclipped the straps of the backpack. His legs immediately swung backward, catching Kent in the crotch with his heel.

—Shit! barked Kent.

—Sorry, Gary said, rolling over and up.

He tried to correct the roll by fanning the boards in the other direction, but the aerodynamics were more complicated than he'd allowed for, and he just saw the girders in the roof swing by again, a little faster.

—Straighten out, man! he heard Kent shout. You're all bunched up. Straighten your arms. Swim, man, don't fucking flap.

—That's easy for you to say, thought Gary. Mister Fucking Flight Controller. He somehow managed to stop revolving, hung there facing up toward the roof.

—I don't want to fall on those girders, he said, having a mild panic attack before realizing that if he fell anywhere it would be in the direction commonly known as down, to the floor. Okay, he said, let's swim, or fly, whatever. He brought the boards together ahead of him, slicing them edge-on through the air, turned his wrists, and swung his arms back, feeling the resistance. The effect was astonishing. He shot forward in a beautiful gliding line, feeling the warm dusty air move past his face, hearing Kent whooping some way off behind him. The roof girders passed beneath him, and the far wall got nearer. He heard Kent shouting, Surf, man, surf! and wondered what the fuck he meant. He thought he better brake a little, so he stretched his arms out, turned the boards against the current, and twisted violently and unexpectedly into a spiraling line for the roof. He was yelling something about feathers when the girder hit him in the belly and he wrapped around it, winded, hearing his wings hit the floor twenty feet below.

—What's that about if God had wanted us to fly? he grunted as Kent loped up.

89

—Should have surfed, Kent said, picking up a board and holding it out in front of him. Deflect the air. Better control.

—And just what makes you the expert in this sort of situation?

Kent looked up at him as if it was just so obvious he couldn't believe he had to tell him.

—We did this before, remember? First time you did acid. Didn't listen to me then, man, and the advice was good. Surf. Wanna try again?

Gary suddenly thought about Gretchen. Shit, she'd be worried.

—We better get back. What time is it? Jesus, three o'clock. Okay, permission to land . . .

He tensed himself for the dive back to the floor, finding a beam to put his feet on.

—What's the matter? said Kent, looking ludicrously foreshortened.

Gary felt clammy. It had hit him, hard and quick. It was as if he'd suddenly woken up to the hideousness of it all.

—I . . . just can't let go, he said, cramped into a knot by fear. Had he slept through everything before? This was terrifying, just heart-stoppingly terrible, and no fun at all. The whole deal was horrifying, all of it. How could he have ever thought it was exciting or enjoyable? What the fuck was he, Gary Wilder, doing hanging from the roof of a derelict building? He started to shake, to shudder, his jaw clacking uncontrollably, and he was making a high-pitched crying sound. He knew his weight was coming back, just knew it. His feet slipped and he slewed around, his legs flailing wildly.

—Hang on, yelled Kent, sprinting for the door. Gary's eyes were screwed shut and he was clenching his jaw to stop it from rattling. The girder bit into his chest as his weight returned, and he gripped it tighter, hooked his chin over it. It felt like he was being pulled out of shape, this voiceless presence inside him, this unseeable shadowy bulk wrenching him back down to earth,

90

dislocating his bones, twisting his muscles. He was in timeless blackness, nothing but this looming force trying to bring him back to earth, and his grip was slipping. His moaning turned into a long rasping howl for help, then drowned in an ear-splitting explosion which filled his head, and a great rending crash as the wall folded inwards and the dozer tilted groaning through the gap in thick billows of blazing sunlit dust, the silver tracks biting into the rubble, the blade rising up under him. Kent cut the motor and leaped from the cab, scrabbling over the broken blocks of wall.

—Just drop, Gar, it's three feet, you can do it, man, open your fucking eyes . . . three feet, man, it'll catch you . . .

A little later, Kent driving the pickup back to Newdale, Gary was beginning to feel foolish.

—I lost it, Kent, I'm sorry . . .

—Those dozers are the easiest to hotwire, man. I mean, where you gonna go, right? Pigs could catch you on foot.

They laughed. Gary tried to think of something to say, asked Kent about the fusebox stash.

—I ate it, man.

—Any good?

Kent turned to grin at him, and the pickup jumped a lane, lots of angry horns sounding.

—I have no fucking idea, man. What a trip.

EIGHT

'So male and miserable . . .'

The door opened a little way and Kent stood there in his shorts. Gretchen felt like driving to Cuba or someplace, but relieved in spite of herself.

—You're back, she said inanely. I saw the truck. Gary okay?

—Oh, sure.

She followed him into the house thinking, Why do I always feel like shouting at guys to take a shower? Why do I get the dirty guys?

—And hey, we've been doing movies. Neat camera.

Kent squinted through a lens made by his finger and thumb and they went into the living room. Gary was floating on his back, his ankle tied to the coffee table leg by a length of green garden twine, his hands behind his head like he was in a hammock.

—Hi, Gretchen. We started already. Don't get mad, huh?

Gretchen looked from Gary, floating five feet up in the air, perfectly relaxed about it, to Kent in his boxer shorts, with a Coors bottle hanging off his thumb, grinning at her.

—Ha ha, said Gary.

—Yes, indeed, said Kent.

Gretchen wrestled with her feelings for a moment, trying to get them in order. Then they got too twisted and she gave up and laughed. She hadn't heard herself laugh like that in quite a while. She thought it sounded stupid and clamped a hand over her mouth. Then Gary laughed at Gretchen and upset his equilibrium. Gretchen pulled him down into the chair and put a pile of albums in his lap. Kent was whistling tunelessly, fooling with the camera.

—Lookee here, Gretchen.

He passed her the camera, pointing to the viewpiece on the stalk. She pushed her hair behind her ear, put the camera to her eye. A little black and white movie of Gary spinning in space. Pushing off from the walls, doing tucks and rolls.

—Beautiful, she said softly.

—At a theater near you, said Kent loudly.

—Let's hope not, hey, Gary? said Gretchen. So, how's your day been?

—We-ell, said Gary, rolling his eyes up, first we hung around a bait shop while Kent had a nostalgia rush, and then I flew around his old man's warehouse and had a nervous breakdown, and Kent got to drive a dozer through the wall. Then after I mopped up all my hot little tears and had a nap with Teddikins Bear we made some home movies of me swinging the house around my head. Just another day at the office.

—Fine. Did anyone see you do anything impossible?

—I don't think so. Just Kent.

Gretchen watched Kent peering into the camcorder.

—So how'd he take it?

—Ask the guy.

—Okay. Kent?

—Uh huh.

—How did you take it?

—Uh, just popped it back.

Gretchen made a face at Gary.

—Well? he said, raising his hands in an Italian-Jewish shrug.

Gretchen told them what she'd been thinking in the car, about how NASA would think it was fake no matter how startling the tape was, in fact the more true to life they made it the more unbelievable they'd find it. And how they wouldn't want to

93

involve the Pentagon even if they didn't think it was fake, because it would mean losing control.

It made sense to Gary. You're absolutely right. What's the percentage for them? This fake business, though, I don't know, you've seen the footage. Look fake to you?

Gretchen shook her head.

—I'm gonna take a shower, said Kent through a yawn.

—But it might look fake to them. I mean, what you're doing is impossible, right? There is no explanation. So they're looking for wires, special effects, anything. Think about it.

—I have been thinking about it, Gretch, on and off, you know, when I haven't been slumbering prettily in my cot.

—I'm sorry. Anyway, here's what we do. Get me in the movie too, so it's obvious it's not a revolving room. I can sort of take part, so I can show them there's no wires or anything.

Gary took a puff on an imaginary cigar, spoke out the corner of his mouth.

—We only pay scale, and it's not a speaking part. Take it or leave it.

She giggled.

—You got a nice laugh, he said. She turned away, pissed with herself for being embarrassed.

—You blushing?

She got a grip on herself, the ice-maiden, and looked at him.

—Fancy yourself just a little bit, don't you?

—Hell, I'm flesh and blood.

They grinned at each other. They could hear Kent singing in the shower.

—This is nice, said Gary. Like *Little House on the Prairie*. The idiot son out in the yard taking a bucket shower . . .

—Maybe more *The Addams Family*.

Gretchen got serious. Can we trust him? I mean, he's a little lopsided in the head, isn't he? It's a complication.

94

Gary sighed, flipped over the top album in the pile on his lap. See this?

Gretchen took the album. The top and bottom seams had split, and she had to catch the heavy slab of vinyl from falling out.

—Original stereo-effect soundtrack, she read aloud. Radiant Pictures presents *Bikini Au-Go-Go* starring Johnny Gillet, Valeria Pietropaolo. The hottest babes and the coolest waves – I really don't know how I missed this one. With ten beatsome hit songs from The Sand Pythons, The Nu-Beats, The Hi-Tones . . . *Beatsome?*

—Except we were already The High by then. Check the picture on the liner.

She turned the album over. The photograph showed some healthy teens frugging on the beach to a wild beat combo with no amplifiers.

—Wow, you're movie stars, and Kent here . . . the other guys? What happened to them?

—Alex is married and in New York. We talk very occasionally. Well, ten years ago, maybe. He's the bass player. Arty type. Bit quiet, never dug the drugs and chicks much.

—Never dug the drugs and chicks much? *Stop it.*

—Sorry, man. The drummer, Randy Deitch, he was hit by a train. His car stalled on a crossing. Girl with him died too. Hard to find a laugh in that for some reason. That happened just after Kent lit out to escape the draft. Anyway, Kent was chewing a whole bunch of acid, that was his job, and the prospect of little yellow men getting his johnson in their rifle sights, that and the band not getting anywhere and everything . . .

—Excuse me? I thought there was a point to this?

—Oh, right. What I'm trying to say. Mainly that Kent and I go way back. And he never ever did anything disloyal or treacherous. Stupid and illegal, sure. But not treacherous. And, you know, I trusted you?

95

—Meaning?

—Meaning I got an eye for people I can trust. Also, it's like routine for the guy, this stuff. Nothing special. He likes the fucking camera more, finds it more interesting. Which is almost as weird as the thing itself, if you see what I mean.

—You miss those days, I bet, Gretchen said.

—You kidding? Can't even remember most of them. Anyway, things change, fall apart, get heavier. 'Sixty-nine was the last year that rated the full twelve months, in my opinion, and that was a terrible year. Terrible year. Really, everything could have stopped after the first Moby Grape album, for all the good it's done. Actually we should have known when *Mad* went black and white. Culture on the skids and mean times just around the corner.

Gretchen shook her head, groaning.

—I can't believe I'm hearing this. You're so negative. I can't believe what you're saying. So male and miserable. Are you really telling me the world should have just exploded or something after the first Moby Grape album? That's ridiculous.

Gary considered for a minute, pursing his lips to aid the thought process.

—I guess you're right. There are a couple of decent songs on the second album.

Gretchen snorted. And what is this, excuse me, bullshit, telling me you don't live in the past. All those albums? Nobody has albums anymore, you can't *buy* them. And those magazines, make the dentist's waiting room look like a newsstand. I mean, do you know what decade we're in?

—What you're telling me, I should listen to rap music and smoke a little crack with the homeboys, right. Get with the times? Wear a knit cap, grow a goatee and call old ladies motherfuckers?

—I just think, I just think, you know . . .

—Yeah, well, you could be right. But I haven't been living in the past so much as being in a kind of sleep the last couple decades. You know, things seem to happen around you, you get tired of trying to hold onto things, you can't change things, you just kind of sleep along through it. Just let it all go. Christ, I'm not nostalgic. There's only one past, and it's the place where everything happens, like it or not. The latest rap record, right, what the fuck that's called, that was recorded in the past. It just wasn't made for me. I'm not nostalgic, just kind of . . . numb. It's all *gone*. Nobody's doing anything that says Gary Wilder, this is for you. Nothing's getting through to me. Now we got Clinton instead of Kennedy, Madonna instead of Marilyn. There you go. Tell me I'm wrong, right?

They were quiet for a bit, Gary feeling first a kind of smug righteousness at having delivered such a resonant state-of-the-union address, and then more and more convinced what he'd said actually meant nothing, that it didn't express what he felt at all. He didn't even know if he had anything he wanted to express. Anything he said now seemed superfluous, anyway. What was there to say?

—Wow, he said. Getting a little heavy there. I've been mouthing off, haven't I? Anything you wanna tell me?

—Like what?

—I dunno. Like why you're with Vandergelder? What's he to you?

She flopped onto the couch, twirling the album.

—It seemed a good idea at the time. I needed to get away from where I lived. He's my uncle. He's nothing to me. Okay?

Gary waited for some more, but nothing came. He tented his fingers under his chin.

—Ve-ry comprehensive . . . I think that about covers it, thank you. But just for our files, did he ever try it on?

Gretchen started to get mad, caught his look, like he was baiting her, backed off.

—I just have this thing for guys in wheelchairs. Call me old fashioned.

97

Kent came in, towel around his waist, dripping water on the carpet.

—Welcome back, said Gary. We've been yakking about old times. Once Gretch and me get going, oh Lord . . .

—Can I borrow some duds? Mine are in the desert, I think. I've put my funeral clothes in the garbage. That's it with shoes, man, they're real sinister, like putting your feet in lizard mouths. You still got that slot car set-up? Hey, *Bikini Au-Go-Go*, far out. Slap it on, man . . .

—You'll find some jeans and a shirt in my bedroom. You're slopping water on the carpet. Wait. I don't give a shit. But use your own underwear, huh, I'm particular about who gets into my shorts. They're Sears, come in the mail.

Kent went to look for some clothes.

—What's that bottle on his thumb? said Gretchen.

Gary feigned bafflement. What bottle?

Gretchen threw a cushion at him.

—Hey! he yelled. Horseplay leads to foreplay.

—Whaaat?

—Our gym teacher said that, the weird fuck. Listen, are we going to make a movie or what? Where's our cameraman? Where's my fucking entourage?

Later, they sat on the floor with the *Bikini Au-Go-Go* soundtrack playing and passed the camera around like it was a bong, watching the little movie of Gary doing his stuff, really quite adept and even graceful, Gretchen holding his belt and twirling him around like the hands of a clock, spinning him like he was on a spit, through her arms to show there were no wires. All the tricks they could think of, including sitting in the chair with the albums on his lap, removing one at a time until he began to rise up in the air. And a nice sequence where he'd push off from a wall, Gretchen catching him, flipping him over, flying back to the wall, doing it again.

—This opens up a whole new source of income for me anyway, said Gary, his legs jammed under the coffee table. Even if NASA could care less, I can get plenty of work as a carnival geek. Wear a propeller beanie and fly around a stripy tent for the rubes.

—Uh, look, it goes backward, said Kent, only it doesn't make any difference. Forward, backward. Weeeeoooo.

—And we need to write the damn letter, said Gary. You got any notepaper?

Girls normally keep that kind of shit. *Darling Muffy, please come to my sleepover, we can toast marshmallows and screech about guys' dicks.* Actually you can use that legal pad under the TV there.

—Just because no-one ever invited *you* to a slumber party, said Gretchen, crawling toward the TV.

—They did, too, said Gary defensively, or they would have done if they'd known what they were. Gretchen sat on the couch, took a Bic from her purse and bent forward to write, clearing a space on the coffee table. He caught a glimpse of the top of her brassiere and the cool shadow between her breasts as her hair fell forward around the paper, over her hand. He wondered if she should be wearing eyeglasses. She stopped writing, lifting the paper up in front of her face.

—Okay. See what you think. *Dear sir, enclosed please find a videocassette you may find of interest. No trickery was involved. The subject is afflicted with a condition of weightlessness and needs sympathetic assistance, without the involvement of the army or the police. If you can help . . .* and here I've kind of stopped. How are we going to set up a meeting?

They thought for a minute.

—He'll probably want to talk to us before he does anything. If he does anything, said Gretchen.

—Yeah. Give him my number here.

—Couldn't he trace it?

—Only with some kind of paperwork from the feds, I think.

We're assuming he won't want to ask for that for a number of reasons, not least that he won't want to get his name on the uh-oh file. He can call with no obligation to buy, listen to us mad guys for free. Give him my number. The hell with it. She finished the letter and read it back to him.

—What a priceless lasting treasure is a college education, he said. My tongue still makes the shape of the letters when I write.

Gretchen looked at her watch.

—Oh my God, oh my God . . . I'm an hour late for Vandergelder. I better go. I'm in trouble. Oh . . . shit.

She got to her feet and hunted for the keys in her purse.

—I'll catch you guys later. If I'm still alive. Listen, give me the tape, I'll send it express, it's safer. I'll get the address from the phone guys.

—Anything we can do?

She looked at them, Gary jammed awkwardly under the coffee table, Kent lying on his back looking in the camera, making little weeeooo sounds. She curled her lip.

—You're kidding?

After she'd gone Kent said, Did you hear that?

—Huh?

—She said shit.

—Bullshit, too. I'm a bad influence.

100

NINE

The Sultan of Strange

—That *asshole*, said Gary, Vandergelder did that? pointing to the bruise on her arm. She nodded.

—I don't know if he knew what he was doing. He was pretty mad. He's just real jealous, it's insane. He was telling me all this stuff, it makes me feel sick. I just left him there at the hospital, it's his hydro today. I'm not going back for him.

—They'll get him a cab?

—I guess so. Jesus. All this time and he's thinking I'm his property or his little girl or something. And he hates you, Gary, he really loathes you, you know that?

Gary shrugged. Kind of hard to care. I'm not exactly going to paint his goddamn porch so he likes me. So what are you going to do?

—Move out, I guess. No way I can stay in the same house now. She rubbed her arm.

—Fetch your stuff, said Gary. You can use the spare room.

Gretchen had anticipated this. She tried to come up with a suitably noncommittal way of accepting.

Gary, reading her hesitation as doubt, said, Just until you get your own place.

That got her off the hook.

—Thanks, Gary. And I better be quick, I really don't want to see the guy again. Ever, if possible.

—Kent, can you give Gretchen a hand with her things?

Kent swung the bottle on his thumb, looking at it curiously. Gretchen rolled her eyes up.

—Oh, I can manage, she said. There really isn't much. Ten minutes.

Back at Vandergelder's she found a cardboard box in a cupboard and put in it the few kitchen things that were hers; a Huckleberry Hound mug she'd had since school, a green glass vase, and her juicer. She went into the living room and looked sourly at the plastic African sculpture, the padded cocktail bar, the massive TV that pulled everything into a stupid wide-screen effect.

Nothing here that she either owned or wanted to see again or that didn't make her sick to her stomach. How had she ever lived here so long? Upstairs, she emptied her closet into the new green ripstop nylon case she'd bought for her dreamed-of move to San Francisco. She rolled her European-style quilt into a plastic bag along with the matching pillowcase, and carefully packed all the odds and ends from her dressing table in the cardboard box. Then she unplugged her bedside lamp and pushed it down into the quilt so the lavender glass shade wouldn't break. In the bathroom, she stuffed her toiletries and cosmetics into a wash bag and put that in the case.

She was carrying everything downstairs, the plastic bag in her teeth, when she heard a car pull up outside. Without wasting time to see if it was Vandergelder, she threw everything out into the backyard. Kent was by the fence, and reached over for the case.

—Can you smell mimosa? he said. I can smell it.

Gary was squinting through a crack in the curtains.

—The cab driver just got the chair out the trunk. He's helping him into it. Jesus, that phony. Should have seen him setting those traps in the yard that time, or standing at my window when I was on the ceiling. Legs more use than mine. Really. Pushing him up the driveway. That's it. He's inside. Expect a neighborly visit sometime soon.

—I gotta go, said Kent, flicking the light switch on and off with his nose. People to see.

Gary and Gretchen exchanged looks.

—There's some cab fare in the ashtray there. Help yourself. Where you going? Coming back?

Kent slumped a little, rubbed the palms of his hands together in circles. He looked thin and empty again suddenly.

—I gotta cut the grass, he said blankly, and walked out.

—Huh? said Gretchen. He's got to cut the grass?

—It's what we used to say. It's just like saying he's got to go, be somewhere else. No particular reasoning behind it. Oh well, he comes and he goes.

Gary wondered if he could take off the weights and have a swim around, but guessed that Vandergelder might be paying a visit soon.

—I just thought, said Gretchen, looking up and flicking the hair from her face, I mean, Kent's gone, right. What if he talks?

Gary laughed.

—Oh sure. Charles Manson grabbing your lapel and telling you to come and see his special buddy who can fly. And you're going to hang around to exchange addresses? I don't think so. Our secret is safer with him than it is with us. Credibility is not a big thing with the guy. Never was, incidentally.

The phone rang, and Gary picked it up. Yeah, oh, hello, Mr Vandergelder.

He made a gagging expression at Gretchen. Uh huh. Uh huh. Like you care, right . . .

—Let me talk to him, said Gretchen, reaching out to take the phone. She held it away from her head, wincing.

—No point in listening to *that*, she said, and dropped the handset back on the hook.

—Nice guy, said Gary. Shame he couldn't come by for pretzels. He unlaced the steel-toed boots and rubbed his feet.

—What did Kent say? Caskets, lizard mouths? Anyway, mind if I take a flight into the kitchen? I'm beginning to want to *do* this stuff, rather than just let it happen to me. If you get my meaning. I was actually even sort of glad when I felt the thing starting up again. If you can understand that. I'm not sure I can.

He shouldered out of his backpack, unclipping the belt just as he turned up and over in the air.

—Yee-haw, he said, in a dry and bored voice. He pushed up to the ceiling and stood there, feet either side of the lamp, with his arms folded, solemn expression on his face.

—I claim this ceiling on behalf of the Untied State of America. Just this little bit round the lamp. Not as far as those cobwebby things over by the shelves but incorporating that crack in the plaster there, I think.

Gretchen giggled. He tried to march around the ceiling, but ended up falling lazily down toward her. She grabbed his ankle.

—Gotcha.

She stood up, pulled him closer, smiling. He held her wrist between his finger and thumb, very gently.

—Maybe I got you.

Their faces were close now.

—Kinda strange, huh? he said softly.

—You could say that.

She let him go, giving him a gentle spin. He curled into a ball, turning over and over.

—What's weird, he said, I don't feel dizzy.

—Not like being in love, then . . .

He swung under the coffee table, flattening his nose unattractively against the glass.

—What?

But she'd already gone, muttering something about sorting her stuff out. Gary floated around the house while she got her

104

room ready. He tried using an album sleeve to fan himself along, thinking you couldn't do this with CDs, incidentally. Once or twice he knocked his head or elbow on the furniture and Gretchen checked if he was okay. Like he was a kid learning to ride a bike. He felt somehow settled. There were no fluctuations in the effect that he could tell, no elevator feelings, just a kind of quiet, playful euphoria. All the panic and terror he'd felt at the warehouse had evaporated with his body-weight. He was perfecting propelling himself from door frame to door frame when he saw Gretchen watching him from her room.

—Really, what a *boy*, she said. First evolutionary step for two billion years and he uses it to see how fast he can get round the house.

Gary swung to a halt in the hall and hung with his hands on his hips, his head on one side, and his feet somewhere near the ceiling.

—Got a better idea?

Gretchen made a face he couldn't decipher upside-down.

—I might have.

He twisted around and held himself upright in her doorway. She'd put her flowery quilt on the bed and tidied the room up.

—Mmm, girlie *room*, said Gary. Today's homes need the cheerful delicacy of a woman's touch.

Gretchen sat on the bed. Her eyes were sly and bright.

—A woman's touch? Fly over here a second, Airboy.

Gary propelled himself forward, luckily getting the distance right and managing to stay upright. She grabbed his shirt.

—Well, she said, I don't know about delicacy. It's been quite a day and I'm too keyed-up to be subtle. Take a shower.

—Huh?

—Don't float there with your mouth open, it looks dumb. Take a shower. Wash your hair. Have a shave. Use some cologne. Make an effort. This is an opportunity you'd be kind of silly not to take, right?

105

Gary grinned. Opportunity? Did she mean what he thought she meant? Did people still do this stuff? Gretchen made a go-on-then-stupid face and pushed him backward.

A new first for Gary Wilder, he intoned, gripping the faucet with his toes to keep himself under the shower. Famed sexual gymnast and celebrity babe magnet Gary 'Wildman' Wilder tonight attempts a zero-g fuck-fest right here in funky downtown Newdale Heights. Maybe not a first, though, women astronauts I think, clipboards floating by, globs of space food. Jesus, my balls feel fantastic, not like the saggy mush they are usually, look at this, for chrissake.

He rolled out of the shower and toweled off, flicked some generic cologne on his face and looked at himself in the mirror. He was a little sunburnt from when he'd lain by the lake. Hey, great tan, Gar. He pulled his stomach in. Women go for the mature bod, triggers a hormone rush they can't control. And a very useful tire-iron boner, like when he was thirteen and getting the kind of spontaneous, tensile hard-ons you could lever up floorboards with. Then he had a moment of sudden doubt so vivid it made him grate his teeth until he could taste his fillings. What if he'd totally misread the situation? It wouldn't be the first time he'd got his glands sizzling like kidneys in a skillet over no flame whatsoever. That little embarrassment with Cindy. There was a knock on the door.

—Need any help?

—I'm not decent.

—Fine. Me neither.

The door opened. Gary held a towel round his waist, coyly, pressing his erection down. Gretchen stood there in her baby-blue underwear. She looked very young, with her narrow hips, her breasts high and small. Her skin had a good, even color, like pale honey.

—See? I'm really not decent . . .

—Indecent exposure, she said, coming toward him. He reached out and pushed the lock of blond hair back behind her ear, slid his hand behind her head, stroked the warm nape of her neck, lifting the weight of her hair. She was looking right in his eyes, smiling, something he found both unsettling and arousing. She took his johnson in her hand, squeezing the towel around it.

—Er, wow, he said hoarsely. This is, er, great.

—I like to get a handle on a man, she giggled, tugging him toward her.

—You are one unusual . . . , he said, and their mouths met. He felt the seams in her brassiere rub his chest, and her hand squeezing his cock, and the rough edges of her teeth on his tongue. He smelled her hair, her warm skin, and the intrusive ugly tang of his cologne. She was walking backward, looking wide-eyed innocent and humming, pulling him by his cock. His arms reached around her neck, his fingers in her hair, sliding down, slipping her bra strap over her smooth-boned shoulder, feeling that delicious tension and release. They came up for air. She shook her hair from her face.

—Just . . . don't do that, that *rutting* routine, right . . . let me . . .

They were in her room now, lit by the lamp with a lavender shade. She held his hips and moved him back, slipping the towel off him, leaving him with the toes of one foot barely brushing the carpet. She took off her underwear without trying to make it erotic, as if she were alone. Gary was floating toward the ceiling, and put his arms up to push back down, but Gretchen held his waist and pulled him down between her legs, holding him between her thighs. He put his hands on her breasts. They felt cool and smooth and somehow unbelievably gentle. Her nipples hardened against his palms.

—You are so beau . . . he began, looking into her eyes, but she took his wrists and twisted his arms behind his back.

107

—Shut up, she said, trailing her fingertips down over his chest. Don't move.

—Oh *God* . . . he sighed, arching over backward, closing his eyes. He felt her pull him up inside her. His legs curled back around hers and he angled his hips up so he could push deeper.

—No, she said, Don't hold me, let go, let me go . . .

He relaxed.

—Whatever, he said. This is kind of new for me. He hoped she knew what he meant. But she hadn't heard. She worked him in and out, slowly, holding his waist. He felt he was going to come, and gasped.

—Wait . . . she said, and lifted him by his hips, easing him out and sliding his wet cock up over her belly, nudging up under her breast, up her neck, into her mouth. His head rocked back, eyes closed, and he moaned. She lifted his legs up so he hung on his back in mid-air, and let go, holding him with just his cock sucked hard in her mouth. She traced a fingernail down over her nipple, twisting it into her breast, and her other hand went down between her legs, her fingers slapping her cunt, poking it, sticking her fingers up inside her. Her nails bit into her breast and she shook it. She began to shudder and moan, her mouth full of his cock as her hand moved faster and they both came, Gary folding forward, saying oh God oh God, taking her head in his hands. She swallowed greedily and messily, kissing the head of his cock, and dropped to her knees and let him go, watching him slowly revolve, his limbs abandoned as if in sleep.

—Well, she said, I hope you remembered to take notes.

They lay on the bed, her arm and leg thrown across to keep him down.

—You're a strange girl, he said.

—*I'm* strange? Excuse me? Don't let's forget what *strange* really is. You're the Sultan of Strange, Gary Wilder.

—But this is our first date.

—What, I'm rushing you? Like you don't kiss on first dates?

—I think I mean you really surprised me. I'd got you pegged as some freckled kid from the mountains, gathering armfuls of showy blooms, a dog called Scamps your most bestest friend.

Gretchen frowned at him.

—Have you been going to pillowtalk classes?

—Just out of practice. What I mean is, you're pretty perverse. I'm surprised.

—You don't know the half of it. Anyway, you really don't know me, so I don't know why you're surprised. You don't have any experience of my behavior to judge me on. You don't know me.

—But I *thought* I knew you, which is the same thing. That's all it takes to be surprised or disappointed or betrayed, you think you got a line on someone.

—Well, maybe I wanted to show you that you don't have a monopoly on surprise.

—That you did. I can't tell you.

Gary turned and looked at her profile. Maybe beautiful, hard to tell.

—Okay, he whispered. Since we're such good neighbors now, what's the big secret?

—You think I'm that mysterious? How flattering.

—Yeah, you got a story to tell. I just know it. You live a secret life, sure you do.

—I tell you, it's the first time I tell anyone. Why should I?

—Well golly gee, Gretchen, I was right about you all along. It's the deal. I told you mine.

He watched her narrow her eyes, thinking out what she was going to say. She took a breath.

—Okay. I killed a guy once.

Gary laughed. Sure you did. With the lead pipe, in the library.

Gretchen carried on as if he hadn't said anything. Her eyes were closed.

109

——He got me pregnant and then he beat me and my baby came out in bits, little bloody bits, and I hit him. With a rock, on the back of the head. In the woods. It was raining. He didn't get up. I may have hit him again. I did.

Gary tried to get this straight. You're not kidding, he said flatly.

——No, I'm not kidding.

——Wow. You're right, you make me just an amateur at surprise. They catch you?

——What do you think, stupid? I went to the chair for this? No, they didn't catch me. They didn't even find him until about a year later. Over a year. I dug him in.

——Who was the guy?

——This good-looking Latino who worked at the school . . .

——Hey, wait a minute. You were at *school*?

——He cut the grass, cleaned the pool. Anything that involved flexing his pecs in his undershirt. Dark hair, buns to stun . . .

——Had all the girls wringing their pants out, huh.

——Oh yeah. It wasn't like I was the only one. He had the run of the roost, you know?

——Yeah, but beating up on you is way out of line. He had it coming.

——Maybe he did, but doing it out of a sense of justice was the last thing on my mind. I didn't know what was on my mind. I wasn't thinking. It wasn't a revenge thing, planned. He beat me up badly so I miscarried, and I hit him back. I'm not proud of it.

——I wouldn't worry about it.

——But you can see why it's not in my résumé.

——Well, it explains a few things.

——It does?

——Like why you're stuck away at Vandergelder's. Low profile, hiding from the world, getting back on your feet. Something like that bound to mess your life up.

—Only temporary, this Vandergelder thing. A little more money in the bank and I was out of here anyway.

—Yeah? You got plans?

—San Francisco. Always wanted to go there for some reason. Thought it would be a good place to start a new life for myself. I don't know.

—Sure it would. Get away from all the shit. New start.

—We're experts at that, huh, Gary? These things happen, and we have to deal with them. Like your wife. What happened? You fool around?

—I would have, if I'd known she was. For sure.

—She left you for someone else?

—Well, she had her reasons, I guess.

—So what were they? A woman doesn't just walk out if everything's perfect. Or tolerable, even.

—I used to peel back her eyelid and lick her eyeball while she was asleep.

Gretchen made a yee-uck sound, but a laugh in there too.

—That's what I *told* her I used to do, anyway.

She turned toward him and kissed his cheek. So, Gary, what miracles are you going to do with this force of yours?

He smoothed back her hair. You think it's a force? I hadn't thought of it that way. It's a weakness.

He swung smoothly out of bed and glided to the door. G-Force. G for Gary. Garavity, he said. I think it'll be easier for you if I fly my own bed tonight. The Sultan of Strange, huh? I like that.

Gretchen mumbled something into the pillow and clicked off the light.

TEN

Pepper on a Rubber Chicken

Sometimes Gary could remember his dreams when he woke up, but not this time. He was more occupied with the tape across his mouth and somebody binding his hands behind his back. An initial thought that Gretchen had snuck into his room and was trying some really weird stuff was killed by a voice he dimly recognized as Vandergelder's, right in his ear.

—What in heck do we have here?

Gary shut his eyes against the stabbing beam of a halogen flashlight and kicked out with both feet, catching something soft. Vandergelder swore quietly and twisted him over, pushed him down on the floor and sat on his back. Gary bucked, flipped like a fish in the bottom of a boat. Vandergelder grabbed his flailing feet and taped his ankles together, wrestled him over, all in a ridiculous muffled silence. Gary stopped struggling, tried to get his breath. Vandergelder's mouth was right next to his ear.

—What have you been *doing* here, Wilder?

Gary grunted as loud as he could with his mouth taped up. Vandergelder pinched his nose hard until he stopped.

—That's better. No need to wake the girl up. We can sort this thing out between the two of us. But I need time to think this through, so we'll take a little trip back to my house. You finished struggling? See, I just have to hold your nose like this . . . that's better.

He got off Gary's back and gave him a little kick, watched him float up.

112

—Light as a feather . . . you're a freak, Wilder. A nasty little freak. And while we're at it . . .

He bent and picked up the roll of tape from the floor, took the end in his teeth and tore off a strip, sticking it over Gary's eyes. Gary heard him chuckle pleasantly.

—One trussed chicken. That what you are, some kind of chicken?

He picked up the flashlight, and guided Gary through the house by his neck. Gary heard the kitchen door open, the familiar sound of the rubber draft seal unsticking . . . had he really left it open? Then the cooler night air, and his back scraping what he guessed to be the fence. He grunted as the metal post grazed his skin, and caught up in his *Bitter? I'm Not Bitter* teeshirt. Vandergelder jerked him free, and Gary felt himself being guided into Vandergelder's house, knocking against walls, doors opening and closing, going down some steps, then being taped to a metal chair. He felt concrete under his bare feet, and the tape was peeled from his eyes. They were in Vandergelder's basement. There were ladders racked on the breezeblock walls and a toolrack and a workbench with old tins of paint stacked up on it. The light came from wire-covered bulkhead lamps on the walls. Vandergelder stood directly in front of him, leaning forward with his hands on his knees. He wore dirty orange plaid slacks, fraying house slippers, and his undershirt clung to his skinny ribs. He said nothing for quite a while, then he went and shook free another metal chair from the stack against the wall, set it up facing Gary. He sat down, Gary hearing the aluminum creak.

—You must have quite a story to tell me, Wilder. He wiped his face with his hand and flicked sweat off his fingers. Only, I'm not interested. I don't have to listen to your nonsense, Wilder. I'm not interested in why you are like you are. I just look at it as . . . an opportunity. I admit, it's not what I expected, I expected to bring back the girl, but I learned a long time ago to be flexible. See, I'm the type of guy who looks at a situation and

113

says, Perry, what can *you* get out of this? How can this situation profit Perry Vandergelder? Do you understand me?

Shut the fuck up, you stupid asshole, thought Gary.

Vandergelder continued, obviously charmed by the conversational tone of his own voice.

—So, when I saw you floating around like some kind of space man, I needed to figure out what's in it for me. So I changed my plans. That's my philosophy. I don't worry my head about the big questions like some folks, why this, why that . . . I just don't see the benefit. Makes the world a much simpler place to live. So I'm looking at old Bob Wilder's son, the chip off the old block, pulling some kind of unnatural stunt, and I'm thinking . . . you know what *I* think? I think I can earn a little money here.

He eased up a skinny thigh and let out a long, animal fart.

—That girl's cooking, really, and then she has the nerve to complain. Yes, old Bob Wilder, now, you didn't know this, up at the old SS and T plant, dear old Bob did everything he could to destroy my life after the accident, took it real personal because it happened on his floor. He had to take a lot of flak for it. He made my life very tricky for a while, just out of spite, or jealousy, maybe. Your dear mother came on to me more than one time, did you know that? Until she took off with that shoe salesman or whoever he was. Takes all types, I suppose. Even a shoe salesman was more fun in the sack than old Bob. Still, when you think where he is now . . .

Vandergelder grinned, showing a lot of small gray teeth, and slapped Gary's face. Gary blew a hot slug of blood out of his nose, grunted, his eyes screwed up tight.

—And where you are . . .

Gary sucked back the blood he couldn't blow out and swallowed it so his breath bubbled through one nostril. His face stung, felt hot and gritty. Vandergelder went to the workbench and picked up a tangle of clothesline, walked behind Gary,

114

unpeeled the tape that bound him to the chair, and tied one end of the clothesline to his wrists. He gave him a push between the shoulderblades that sent him tumbling forward, and jerked back on the rope like it was a leash. Vandergelder laughed as Gary spun back, knocking the chair over with his head.

—This really is the most fun since . . . well, I can't tell you.

He jerked the rope again, and the back of Gary's head bounced soundlessly off the floor. Vandergelder reeled him in, put a foot on his chest. Gary's eyes were closed, and his breath whispered weakly through his nose.

—Oh dear, Vandergelder said softly, rocking him with his foot.

Gary was gone, a long way away, swimming through green water, hunting for his Captain Midnight watch. He could see it glinting on the sandy bottom amongst the weeds, only it kept moving. Somebody had it on a string. He was swimming with his hands behind his back, moving along by undulating his whole body. The watch jerked away, and it was dark and cold, and he couldn't breathe. His lungs were bursting, blood banging in his temples. He tried to shout for help but his mouth was full of rotten weeds. Water sucked up into his nose. He blew it out.

—Oh dear. Vandergelder's voice, strangely echoey. Gary opened his eyes and it was like looking through a bloody soap bubble. Vandergelder ripped off the tape over his mouth, and Gary sucked in a great draft of dizzying air, let it go. His mouth felt like pepper on a rubber chicken.

—*Fuck* you, Gary gasped, his voice faint and harsh.

Vandergelder laughed. You really must learn some manners.

Gary kicked out, flying back against the toolrack on the wall. Winded but thinking clearly now, he felt the saw blade cut against his wrists, worked the teeth over the tape, slicing it easily, felt the clothesline catch and fray. Old stuff, and rotten. Vandergelder wasn't laughing now, coming toward him. Gary's hands snapped free and he kicked back against the wall, flew at

Vandergelder, grabbed his throat with one hand, his face with the other, gouging his eyes. He twisted right up over behind his head, Vandergelder spinning round squealing, trying to get a grip on Gary's arm, catching a wrist. They crashed back against the toolrack, fell, Gary underneath. He grabbed the hammer fallen from the rack and brought it up against the side of Vandergelder's head, no room for a backswing. The guy sagged. Gary kicked out from under him and drifted away, ripping the tape from his ankles. He pulled himself toward the stairs by a pipe running along the ceiling, floated up the steps, grabbed the door handle as he heard Vandergelder yell. The hammer hit his shoulder and clattered back down the steps. He wedged himself up against the ceiling and twisted the handle, fumbled the door open, pulled himself through, feeling pain flame into his shoulder. Vandergelder on the bottom step now, picking up the hammer. Gary crouched on the wall above the door, knees touching the ceiling. Just ahead of him the dull gleam of a window. He held his breath and kicked as hard as he could, covering his head with his arms, shattering straight out through the glass into the night.

ELEVEN

Teenage Tidiness Patrol

Want to see something weird?

Cy Scott had entered without knocking again, like it was just the mail room and not an office. He was waving a UPS package that Wyndham Lennox bet contained a videocassette.

—This is a *goody*, growled Cy. Read this while I set it up.

He thrust a letter into Lennox's hand, on yellow legal paper. The handwriting didn't look crazy, anyway. In common with most high-profile national and international organizations, NASA was flooded with mail from the kind of people who got faded out during phone-in shows. UFO nuts, conspiracy theorists demanding the truth about the faked Apollo moon landing, psychonutbars ranting about wasting taxpayers' money when the sidewalk needed patching. This was Wyndham Lennox's job, up there in the Unsolicited Communications office, dealing with the mail no-one had asked for, binning it, mostly, or drafting replies as appropriate, sometimes assigning it to an individual or department if, on further investigation, it warranted it. Or he felt nasty. He also dealt with inquiries too routine or too generic to be attractive to anyone else, and took phone calls too persistent for the switchboard team to have the time to fend off. But it was the flake mail that made the work interesting, the elaborate handwritten files in shoe boxes, the blurry snapshots of Aliens from Outer Space, the charred bits of metal, the big poster-size sheets of interlocking symbols and star maps, sometimes quite beautiful. But all as flaky as an Italian car.

—*Dear sir*, he read aloud, that's okay so far, at least it's not written in fingerpaint, *enclosed please find a videocassette you may find of interest.* Aha. *No trickery was involved. The subject is afflicted with a condition of weightlessness*, blah blah, blah bl . . . Lennox's voice tailed off.

—Ready? Cy swung the monitor of the big Grundig around and rolled up a chair next to Lennox. He stabbed the play button. Thirty minutes later he turned to him, grinning, and said, Well?

Lennox took off his clip-on necktie and carefully rolled it up into a clean mug he kept on his desk for just that purpose. He loosened the collar of his white short-sleeved shirt and nodded his head.

—Sharp stuff. Either it's the real thing, or it's a state-of-the-art computer-aided simulation. So I guess that's what it is.

He rolled the tape back, froze it.

—Look at this. The guy increases the speed of rotation by going into a tuck, slows it by straightening out. Classic zero-g configuration. Question is, why would a bunch of professionals send us a very expensive little movie and pretend it was a home videotape? That's the real mystery here.

—Some kind of publicity scam, maybe. Some of those FX guys having a little fun.

They ran it through a second time, looking for wires, trickery, anything. Lennox tapping the screen with his pencil during particularly 'sharp' maneuvers. They played sections of it in slo-mo, and some backward, which curiously enough made no difference to much of it.

—Anyone else seen this? Lennox said, watching the guy with the army haircut spin through the woman's arms.

—Nope. Came through to me, for some reason. I gave it a quick spool through in conference three while I drank my coffee, brought it right up. Definitely your area.

118

Lennox peered at the letter through the rimless glasses his wife said made him look old. He *was* old, dammit.

—There's a phone number here, right, he said, turning it over, but no address. I could give, what's this scribble? I can't make it out, I could give her a call.

—You're sure it's a her?

—Oh sure. The handwriting. I reckon it's the blonde in the movie. Want to hang around?

—I got meetings. Ciao. Have fun.

Lennox kicked the door shut after him and ran the tape through again. He should really show this to Special Projects. If it was kosher, of course. He didn't want to waste their *valuable* time on a hoax, though. He dialed the number in the letter. It rang twice and then a woman's voice said hello as if it was a question.

—Yes, hello, this is Wyndham Lennox from NASA? I'm calling from the public services department. You submitted a videocassette?

—It arrived, huh. Thank God.

—Well, you paid UPS a fair sum of money to do the job, maybe you should thank them. Would you mind telling us a little more about it, when it was taken, where it was taken? Things like that? Do you have the time to talk right now or should I call back? I'm sorry but I couldn't make out your name.

There was a pause.

—Gretchen. Just Gretchen. Listen, we have a small problem concerning the guy on that tape. That's me with him, by the way. On the tape.

—You have a problem?

—Yeah. We sure do. We lost him. Last night.

—You lost him? I don't understand.

Lennox heard the tension in the woman's voice when she answered.

—He wasn't in his bed. He's not in the house, and the back door was open. I'm on my own here now, and I don't know what to do. Kent's gone, God knows if he'll be back . . .

—Kent?

—Yeah, Gary's friend?

—Gary's the guy in the movie.

—Yeah.

—Listen, Gretchen? Gretchen, maybe he just went out for a walk or something.

—Did you watch the tape or not? I mean, Jesus, the guy can't walk a single step. He's weightless.

—Okay, so maybe it's worn off and he's okay, and he's gone to take some air.

—I don't think so.

—Then you should call the police. Missing persons.

—Mr Lennon, listen to me, listen to me. Gary has somehow flown out of the house like a bird, and you expect me to ask the police to send a chopper after him or something? Why do you think we sent the tape to NASA? Is there anyone else there I can speak to? What's your position there?

Lennox took a breath and smiled as he replied because it softened the timbre of his voice.

—Okay, okay. I understand what you're telling me. I'm the officer in Unsolicited Communications. Wyndham Lennox, that's Lennox. Your package has come to me because this correspondence has yet to be assigned. It is my job to follow it up to a certain level, and then pass it to the relevant department if I think it's appropriate. But I really need more information. We get a lot of unsolicited requests for assistance, involvement, funding . . .

—You think we want money?

—I don't know what to think yet, Gretchen. Here in Houston it's ninety in the shade and the airconditioner in my office doesn't work too well. I'm a slow thinker at the best of times. Now, would you like to back up a little, fill in a little background detail? Then I'll see what we can do.

Lennox listened as Gretchen gave him a pretty lucid account of the last three days. He made a few notes in pencil in the margin of the letter and interjected the occasional ah-hah and uh-huh. The woman sounded sane to him, not that he was qualified to judge in a medical sense, he'd just been around long enough to recognize what he termed a sharp cookie when he came across one. And he liked the tone of her voice. She wasn't trying to get any tiresome polemic over, and she sounded genuinely concerned for this Gary guy.

—Okay, Gretchen, I'll level with you. There are two ways to play this. I can thank you for your interest and promise to get back to you, or I could work on the premise that everything you say is true, and check it out. Maybe a half-dozen times a year I get out on a field trip somewhere, poke around some burnt soil with the toe of my shoe, get an interview on tape, drink a few beers with the locals and hear crazier stories than the one that brought me out there, and plane back to make a report. And I have to say most of them lead to nothing. That's not actually true. In the years I've been doing this job, not a single one has led to anything. There's nothing we can do except make some sort of record of it, put it in the Special Projects filing cabinet. But yes, I'm interested. Mainly because you sound as baffled by this as I'd expect to myself. You're not telling me how or why. But I'm not convinced, I'm *interested*. You say no-one else knows anything about this? No other copies of the tape, ah, floating about?

—You can understand it's been real difficult telling anyone about this. Who do you tell? You're like the only chance we have at the moment. You have the only copy of that tape. When can you get here?

—Where's here?

*

121

Lennox watched Annie pack his suitcase for him, folding his shorts and socks with the absent-minded care that forty years of marriage makes automatic.

—I really don't see why you have to go flying off all over the place just because someone's made a clever little movie. Well, anyway, you'll need a spare jacket, I'm packing your sand linen, and there's plenty of socks under your shirts here. Have you got your hygiene bag ready?

Lennox pulled her onto his lap.

—Still a little too skinny to be really attractive.

He kissed her ear. Maybe get me a nice surfer girl in a French bikini while I'm out there.

Annie smiled, patted his hand and stood up, pulling the hem of her skirt straight.

—That would be nice, dear. Should I pack your earplugs for you? Hotels can be awfully noisy.

Lennox unpeeled himself from the plastic chair in arrivals at LAX. He'd recognized the pale hair falling over one eye, a little like Veronica Lake on a bad day. With no makeup and wearing stonewashed jeans, a sleeveless blue top that showed her midriff, and pink canvas deck shoes. He waved the copy of *Time* magazine they'd agreed would be the signal, just like they were spies, and she came over.

—Mr Lennox?

She looked anxious, and pushed her hair behind her ear. She was much shorter than he'd expected.

—Gretchen? Hello. Wyndham Lennox. Nice to meet you.

Her handshake was right, too, Lennox noticed. Pressure, humidity, duration, animation, all the subtle signals so useful to getting a quick reading of a character. Whether they had any self-confidence, racial hangups. Women tended to think of shaking hands as a guy thing, maybe an excuse for the guy to demonstrate superior male strength, so they were usually much

122

more reserved. Gretchen took his hand without thinking, saying, I think I parked in a towaway zone, we should hurry, if you don't mind. Thanks for coming out.

After a brief altercation with a guy in a blue uniform over where she'd parked, Gretchen keeping her head, staying calm but firm, they climbed up into the cab of the battered pickup and joined the crawl of traffic out onto the freeway.

—Newdale's a couple hours' drive, she said, crunching a gearchange. Shit. Excuse me. This is Gary's truck. Takes getting used to.

—Newdale, huh? said Lennox.

—Heard of it?

—Not exactly. So tell me, the guy, Gary? He's still missing?

—He's still gone. Now I don't know now why I got you out here. There's nothing I can show you. I feel like I've got you out here on false pretenses, I'm wasting your time.

—I wouldn't worry about it. I'm attending a conference in LA. So I'm really killing two birds with one stone, so to speak.

She turned to look at him. You're kind of different to how I thought.

Lennox chuckled, patting back his dull silver-gray hair. Shucks, us black folk can't work for NASA?

—I don't mean that. You're sort of older, is what I mean. I'm being rude, I'm sorry. But you do look kind of military, you know?

—Stays with you, I guess. That's my background. Captain in the Teenage Tidiness Patrol. Then a flyboy. Then training at NASA.

—What, you trained pilots?

—Nooo. I trained to be an astronaut.

—You're kidding? Really?

He wasn't so old he didn't get a kick out of telling the story to a young woman on occasion.

123

—I trained okay, but all I ever got to fly was a desk. Many are called, few are chosen.

—Wow. Don't you regret it?

—What, not going to the moon? Sure I regret it. Like everyone else who didn't go.

—So you're doing this, what, unsolicited communications stuff?

—Part of public services. My last year. I retire next summer. It's a weird way to end a career, I can tell you. So I'm not what I'd imagined, either. So don't worry about it. But I'm not here to talk about me.

He unzipped his flight bag, took out the heavy Sony Professional Walkman tape recorder, with 'NASA property' routed into the black plastic.

—Do you mind? We have to start sometime.

Lennox spoke the date into it, checked the recording level.

—From the beginning?

Gretchen took it slow and careful, retelling the story, leaving out the complications with Vandergelder. Who was where, incidentally? His car not in the driveway. She kept to a steady fifty miles an hour in the nearside lane, telling the story, wondering how many times she'd have to tell it. Up ahead, a hitchhiker.

—Jesus. Excuse me, she said, I think I . . .

She pulled off onto the hard shoulder. The hitchhiker running toward them, thumb out, green glass bottle balanced upright on it, glinting in the sun.

TWELVE

Pink Aluminum (Instrumental)

Gary spun, nothing in his mind but a panic instinct to catch something, anything, to break what felt like a fall, but it was a fall out and up. His foot kicked something, a trashcan lid clattered, the back of his hand brushed the fence, but it was gone. The whole gray earth swung over and around, yellow lights, a barking dog, then the sharp scratch of twigs over the back of his head, a spastic twist and grab, but that chance missed too.

He let his body go limp, watching the Main Street lights swing slowly over his head, and the stars wheel up under his feet. Now the sodium lighting on Beach Street, and the Your Favorite, the yellow light spilling out onto the sidewalk. Working out his trajectory was hopeless, his internal compass was shot to bits. He held his hand out in front of him, saw its dim outline, the lights pass between his fingers. The air was cool, and it was quiet except for the slack rubber whir of distant traffic. His body was one big ache, one dumb heavy hurt. His head hurt the most, so he categorized that first, moved on. The cuts on his wrist stung and his shoulder throbbed, and it felt like he'd caught his heel breaking through the window, and his nose was clogged with blood. His spin seemed to have virtually stopped.

He was flying on his side, the stars at his right hand, the lights of Newdale in a constellation to the left. So he was still going up. Wherever that was. He flew out into the night sky, thoughtless, wide-eyed, flew out and away, not recognizing anything now, trackless, drifting, lost. All his hurt seemed increasingly flat and distant as he looked at the tiny lights, the glittering tinfoil freeways, the magnesium powder cities flaring against the black edge of the ocean, ribboning tinsel veins, the stars outshone. It was cold, and he hung transfixed, his head filled with distance and glitter. There was something increasingly calming about being helpless. There was nothing he could do, no decisions he could make, no direction he could take. He'd always been in some kind of orbit around people and events, at a distance, passive, letting it all happen around him. Hanging up here felt almost comfortable, natural, letting his thoughts swing about his head.

He thought about the people he knew, about his family. The image of him sitting on the porch with his parents seemed archetypal, eternal, carven in time, and yet uneasy. There he was, little Gary Wilder, a tin plane in his hand, peering through the blue acetate cockpit window at the pilot printed flat against a tin seat. His mom staring straight ahead, her mouth grim. His dad on a hard kitchen chair, shifting uncomfortably, tapping his shoes together, taking his handkerchief out and blowing his nose. Nobody speaking. A silence so oppressive he remembered the headache it had given him. It had made his guts clench. His mother hadn't been there even then. Just a paper-thin husk full of dust, colder than space, emptier than space, quieter than space. Little Gary turning the propeller on his tin plane, holding it up to the sky, one eye closed. One family tableau. Gone sour, gone wrong. Think about the tin plane, the blue window. The balloon. The blue balloon. His mom jerking his arm right up like that. The only blue childhood sky he could remember, and the bright balloon sailing up into it.

It struck him as suddenly strange, fantastic, unbelievable, that he had no memories of a happy childhood; no sunlit, laughing pictures of the loving family. A picnic, surely, his dad teaching him how to swing a baseball bat? His mom in the shade of a tree,

126

laughing, cutting sandwiches? Surely they did that? His dad
always got mad when Gary couldn't remember things they'd
done, places they'd been. These memories, where were they?
Just misfiled or never written to begin with? Where was
everybody? This was where the story ends. For no reason. There
was no reason. No explanation. Nobody was telling him anything.
There was nothing to tell. He was a side-effect, a peripheral. The
centre, the warm centre where things happened, was somewhere
else.

From nowhere, he thought he overheard dim snatches of
conversation, getting louder now. His father asking for something. What? Gone. Marcie on the phone, her voice brittle with
static, Kent, laughing right up close, right inside his ear, but
none of this to him, he wasn't included. The voices were talking
to each other. They surged together in a murmuring, rumbling
wave. Flashes of laughter, a shout of anger, now hissing, now
silence.

Gary unclenched his fists, breathed out. The air was so cold,
ice cold. He was shuddering uncontrollably, his teeth rattling.
He kept stuttering, Jesus, Jesus, over and over, just loud enough
to hear himself. He bunched up, hugging his legs to his chest,
every breath a gasp for life. Everything hurt again. Ahead of him,
a vertical frost-blue seam, the sun's widening thread, and the
lovely curve of the earth. He noticed his orientation had changed,
and as the sky paled he felt the air move gently past him and
realized he was falling.

—I am dead, sweet Jesus, I am dead. Had he spoken? He
couldn't tell. The air was getting warmer, slipping over him like
a sheet. The lights below spread, winked out. Shapes became
distinct as roads, suburbs, divided by dark lozenges of forest and
field and the spreading wash of sunlight blurred inky shadows
into the mist. Tiny cars, toy houses, everything unfamiliar. He
was falling faster now, and instinctively swerved into a skydiver's
pose, the air cracking his clothes like whips. This wasn't Newdale

anymore; a quilt of fields, a silver lake, some scattered buildings, an aluminum roof, pearl pink in the sunlight, some farm buildings now alarmingly close, little figures in blue and red flying black flags of shadow across a yard. Gary tucked himself into a roll, the earth flashing around and around him, a blur now, screaming, unheard.

THIRTEEN

Neon Sour Gummi Worms

Laura Somerville grabbed her dad's sleeve and pointed up.

—There's someone falling out of the sky, Dad.

He looked vaguely where she was pointing, willing to go along with the joke.

—Yeah, there he goes, he said, pointing to the wrong place.

Laura stamped her foot, jerked his sleeve again, harder.

—No, Daddy, there, look . . .

He craned his head back, saw a black shape turning high above them, a skydiver, spreadeagled against the pale early-morning sky.

—Oh my God, he said. He's left it too late . . . he should open his chute . . .

Laura jumped up and down on the spot, biting her lip.

—Look look look, he's going over the woods, by the lake . . . come *on*, Daddy . . .

She ran off, still looking up. Ford Somerville stood there a moment. Something was weird about this. He scanned the sky for a plane, listening. Nothing. Now the guy had bunched into a ball. Ford could see his white legs, bare legs, the guy was spinning over and over, went behind the trees beyond the barn. He heard a long, wailing scream, and then a splash.

—Well, at least he didn't dent the barn . . .

He walked slowly over to the woods, calling after Laura to wait. He caught up with her at the gate, jumping up and down, waving her arms.

129

—Did you see him? Did you hear him? He fell in the lake, he fell in the lake . . .

He put his hand on her shoulder.

—Listen to me, Laura, he may be hurt. He may be hurt bad. Run back to the house and get Mom to bring a blanket. Be quick, now.

She frowned up at him, sighed heavily, her shoulders dropping, said *okay*, and ran off, all skinny legs and arms. Ford unhooked the wire loop on the gate post and went into the woods. This was the darnedest thing, as his old man would have said. Feller falling out of the sky like that. Spooked all the birds up again. Things were always being *spooked*. He walked the dirt path between the trees to where he could see the lake, a strip of silver so bright it blurred the trees on its bank. He stood still a moment, listening. The birds were quieting down. He heard water move, over to his left, and a low groan. He went off the path, feet squashing into the pulpy dark loam beneath the trees. There he was, like a hog in the mud at the water's edge, head bowed. Ford walked straight in, got the guy under his arms and pulled him free, the mud making sucking noises. He pulled him up onto a springy patch of grass, and waited for him to stop coughing up water. He read the faded words on his mud-caked shirt, *Bitter? I'm Not Bitter*, without wondering what it meant.

—I can't say if you're the luckiest or the unluckiest guy alive, feller, but at least you're alive. Be a blanket along soon, just get your breath.

Gary started to shiver again, even in this little strip of sunlight. Ford heard Laura and Marie coming through the wood, Laura's excited little voice.

—Over here, he said, raising his head so his voice would carry. In a minute he saw Marie peering through the trees, looking concerned.

—He's okay, he said. A little shook up. You got the blanket?

130

Laura burst out of the woods trailing it behind her, ran down to the strip of grass. She always had to carry everything. He took the blanket and laid it over Gary, dried his face with a corner of it while Laura and Marie stood by, quiet and concerned.

—Thanks, said Gary, in a whisper.

—What's your name? asked Laura.

Ford put his fingertip on her lips. Don't go pestering the feller with questions, now. He turned back to Gary, noticing a little color returning to his cheeks.

—Soon as you've warmed through, we'll think about getting you back to the house. Reckon you've broken anything?

Gary moved his head from side to side. No. I'm okay. Cold. Sorry.

—Nothing to be sorry about, said Ford. Gary looked at his face. A younger guy who looked older, he reckoned, and his wife and daughter, both dark-haired and pretty. Little girl wearing a red cotton print dress, father in blue dungarees, black mud up to the knees. Red and blue. He remembered falling, red and blue figures, and a pink roof.

—Where am I? he said, through a cough.

The farmer guy looked at him, puzzled. Elbow Lake. But let's get you back to the house, if you're set.

He bent and put an arm under Gary's shoulders, lifting him to a sitting position.

—You okay?

Gary nodded. Ford helped him to his feet, Marie taking an arm. Ford looped his other arm over his shoulders, taking his weight.

—What can I do? said Laura.

—Pick up the blanket. Let's get it round his shoulders, there we go.

They went slowly back through the woods, Laura in front, holding back branches for them, opening the gate, leading them

131

across the big yard to the house, a wood house painted white with shingles on the gable end. She leaped up the steps to the porch and opened the front door.

—Jesus, thought Gary dully, I've landed on the fucking Waltons.

He sat by the stove at the big kitchen table, wrapped in the blanket, a big mug of coffee cradled in his hands.

—I can't thank you guys enough, he said, his voice still hoarse.

Little Laura sat right opposite him, peering at him, her mouth twisting from side to side. Marie stood at the stove, stirring something, frowning at this man from the sky with the army haircut. Ford leaned back on the windowsill, rubbing the head of a big black dog who'd just woken up.

—Well, Ford said, you could start by telling us . . .

And it was at that point that Gary blacked out, slumping sideways off the chair onto the floor.

—Want some of these?

Gary opened his eyes. Everything was blurred and sunny, like a sanpro ad. He was in a beautiful soft bed, with heavy cotton sheets, the furry kind. Sunlight shone through the bright yellow flowery curtains.

—Huh?

—You want some of these?

The little girl, what was her name, he knew her. In focus now. Holding out a bright packet of something. He got up on his elbow, feeling the stubble on his chin. He was wearing pajamas, something he hadn't done since Eisenhower. And there was a neat dressing around his wrist. Laura. That was it. He'd fallen into Asshole Lake, he remembered now.

—Uh, what are they?

—Gummi Worms, she said, her whole face distorted with chewing.

Gary flopped back onto the pillow. I guess not, thanks. Got any bourbon?

Laura shook her head, uhn *uhn*.

—Laura, come out of there right this instant.

Marie came in, carrying a pile of laundry.

—You're awake, she said flatly. Laura, run and play.

Laura grabbed the packet off the bed, stuffed another Gummi Worm in her mouth, and skipped out.

—How are you feeling?

Gary thought, all the better for seeing you, in your white blouse with your underwear *just* showing through it if you looked hard.

—Okay . . . a little weak. Hungry, too, I guess.

—Well, I'm not surprised. You surfaced a few times and took some milk, but I guess you don't remember.

He grimaced. I drank some milk? Damn right I don't remember. Are you sure it was me?

—Doctor said you were suffering from exposure and exhaustion . . .

—But my hemorrhoids are cured?

—If you're better we'll get you home, if you tell us where it is.

—Newdale. Newdale Heights.

She shook her head. Meant nothing to her.

—I've brought you some of Ford's clothes. You're about the same height. Your own are in that plastic bag there.

—Ford? Um, thanks. Do you have a phone?

She gave him a quick glance, put the clothes on the chair.

—We have a phone. And running water. Even out here. When you're dressed come down for something to eat. Ford'll be back for lunch any minute. You can tell us who you are and

133

how you came to be falling out of the sky in your underwear, if you can remember *that*.

She left, shutting the door behind her, leaving Gary thinking she was a little cold toward him, wondering why. He got out of bed, grabbing the bed as he realized he was taking his weight for granted. He breathed a sigh of relief, feeling the mattress give beneath him.

—Airboy comes to earth, he said, planting his feet firmly on the polished bare boards.

Downstairs in the kitchen, Gary in a gray workshirt, plimmies, and a pair of jeans a size too small, top button undone, sitting at the table again, wolfing down a ham on rye and a bottle of beer. Ford came in through the side door, wiping his boots on the mat, then taking them off and leaving them by the door, the dog sniffing at them, wagging its tail. Ford looked at Gary, went to his wife doing something wholesome with vegetables in the sink, and gave her a kiss.

—So, he said, turning to Gary, you're up and about. Have a good sleep?

Something about his attitude, thought Gary, cooler somehow.

—Yeah. Thanks. I really mean that, he said, through a mouthful of sandwich.

Ford pulled out a chair, swung it around and sat astride it, folding his arms on the back.

—We don't even know your name. Let's take it from there, huh?

Laura's voice came from outside, calling, Mommy, Mommy. Marie dried her hands on a dishcloth and went outside.

—You should know, said Ford quietly, waiting for the door to close, that you said some pretty filthy things to my wife while you were, ah, unconscious. Now under the circumstances, I'm not going to do anything about it. But you should know what you did. She's looked after you and all you've done is talk dirty

134

and put your hand on her. So you should understand you're not the most welcome of house guests here.

Gary had stopped chewing. So that was it. He swallowed the sandwich with difficulty.

—I'm real sorry, uh . . . Ford?

Gary reached his hand across the table and Ford shook it, looking him in the eye, expressionless.

—Mr . . . ?

—Wilde . . . began Gary, thinking fast, Danny Wilde.

—Okay, Mr Wilde, how about telling me how you come to be dropping out of the sky onto my land? I'm kind of curious.

Gary lined up the crumbs on the tabletop with the edge of his hand, playing for time.

—There was this party, friend of mine in LA, has a Piper Cherokee? I guess we got a little out of it. I was climbing out on the wing, doing a stunt thing. Crazy, right? He dipped the wing, I don't know why, fooling around, and I slipped off. Could have happened to anyone. Anyway, nothing like a cold tub to sober a guy up, right? Jesus, I better call the guy . . . he'll think I'm dead or something . . .

—Phone's in the hall, said Ford. Gary said thanks, finished the beer. The phone was on a little wooden table painted white with an old dark wood chair by it. Lots of pictures in the hall. Black and white prints, photographs of rocks and shit. He dialed his own number and Gretchen answered, Hello, like she was seeing if there was anyone in the cellar, sort of scared.

—Gretch? Jesus, it's good to hear your voice.

—Gary? Gary? Is that you?

He noticed Ford watching him from the kitchen.

—Thought I'd died, huh?

—Where are you? What the hell happened? I've been going out of my mind, worrying . . . thank God you're okay . . .

—No, I'm fine. I'm at . . . where is this again, Ford?

—Somerville Farm, Elbow Lake, said Ford from the kitchen.

135

—Out at Somerville Farm, Elbow Lake.

—Where's that? I never heard of it.

—Ford? Where is that, exactly, in relation to LA, say?

—In relation to California, it's in Utah, said Ford dryly. Just across the state line, take a left a mile out of Saint George. It's signposted.

Gary went dumb, looking down at the phone.

—Some party, wasn't it, Mr Wilde? said Ford.

Gary heard Gretchen's voice, like an insect trapped in the handset, lifted the phone to his face.

—It's in Utah, he said. Yeah, I know. Utah. Take a left after, um, Saint George. Just over the state line. Signposted.

The line was quiet for a while, then she repeated what he'd just said, as if she was writing it down, and asked if he was okay again.

—Yeah, I'm fine. Luckily I fell into a really *nice* guy's lake. Not like those other lakes I fell in where they called me names and pinched my arm. They've been looking after me. Getting my weight back up, so to speak. When can you get out here?

—We're leaving now. In your truck.

—Sure. We?

—The guy from NASA. Kent's around someplace. Anything I should know?

—Well, it's the last time I get into a plane with you, drunk or sober, he said loudly. Get here quick. I've put these good people to enough trouble as it is. Take care now.

He hung up, and went back into the kitchen, rubbing his stubble.

—Utah, right? How far is that from LA?

—I never go there. Not since I did my doctorate at UCLA. But I guess it's something in the order of three hundred miles, I really have no idea.

Right, thought Gary. Knock off about a hundred from Newdale, two hundred miles. They'd be here today.

—Doctorate, huh, he said. You're a doctor?

—Not the kind that diagnoses exposure. After a fall from a plane. Most people who fall out of planes get broken necks. You get exposure. Anyway, we'd better get Roy over. I'll give him a call. He's developed quite an interest in you. Be glad to put his mind at rest.

—Roy? The doctor?

—Roy Gates. Saint George Police. And the *Witness* is running a story on you. Word gets around quick out here. Quite a celebrity. If you want to shave for your picture you can use my spare kit in the bathroom. In the window. Don't use the Gillette in the rack.

—Shave, sure . . .

Give him time to think, and his damn beard itched. He waved a hand at Ford and climbed the stairs, thinking, what's a damn doctor doing as a fucking farmboy, a doctor who couldn't diagnose a fucking metal leg. Named after a car. But so was Lincoln, I guess. All that shit about what I said to his wife, what is she, Mother Teresa? So I made a play for her. Even while close to death I made a play for her. They should be flattered I showed an interest.

The climb up the stairs had made him breathless. In the bathroom he gave himself a shave with the Gillette in the rack, thinking he looked like an old man, his face pale and creased like the paper you found in your grandmother's underwear drawer. He heard Ford's voice, talking on the phone, and edged the door open, holding the handle tight so it didn't make a noise.

—. . . about it I still don't like. I'm not certain that it's his real name, either . . . yes . . . sure. Soon as you can, Roy.

—Smart guy, thought Gary. Thought I'd swung that one past him nicely. Okay, I have to get out of this place, meet Gretch on the road. I do *not* want to see this Roy Gates, or have my picture in the paper. Shit, told what's-her-name I lived in Newdale. No worry. Biggish place. Should not have told her

137

anything. Maybe she won't remember. Can't trust these farm-boys, inbred. Like that film with Burt Reynolds, *Smokey Goes Bananas*, he gets raped by hillbillies.

He rattled the door handle, and came out on the landing. Ford?

Ford standing in the hall, reading a newspaper, looking up now.

—I think I'll take a nap if that's okay with you. Wake me up when your guy gets here.

—Roy's on his way. He has to stop off, but I expect him in about twenty minutes. Don't worry, I'll wake you.

Gary went into the bedroom and shut the door. Twenty minutes? And farmer Ford standing guard in the hallway? He went to the window and opened the curtains. The red tile roof sloped away to the back of the house, a drop of about ten feet to the garden. Laura out there, skipping round an apple tree, singing something.

—Kid should be at school. No sign of what's-her-name. This is the way to go. Hell, I can drop ten feet, I've dropped ten thousand before, no problem.

He pulled up the sash window, put a leg through, grunting. Laura still skipping and singing. He ducked through the opening and sat on the roof, hot tiles under his hands. What's-her-name, he thought, somewhere in the house, calling her daughter in. Don't look up, kid, don't look up, honey, just scamper on by, that's it . . .

—What you doing up there, mister?

—Resting. In the sun, Gary whispered.

—You're not supposed to play on the roof.

—Oh, *right*. I didn't know. Please don't tell on me, huh? Just getting a little sun.

Laura's name called again.

—Well, okay, she said, sounding not sure about the deal, screwing her face up, and skipped round the corner.

Gary shuffled down the tiles and hung his legs over the eaves. Maybe not even ten feet at that. Land in that bed of petunias, what the fuck they are. He was just tensing himself for the jump when he felt a very slight but familiar tingling, all through his body.

—Holy fucking shit.

He brought his heels up on the gutter and jumped into the garden, landing on the big black dog sleeping unseen in the shade. It awoke to find Gary clasping it lovingly around its neck, and saying good boy, nice dog, and rubbing its warm woolly head. This was what Gary had seen Ford do in the kitchen. Before Gary could think of what he was going to do next, the dog staggered to its feet, wagging its tail, and Gary grabbed its collar.

—Attaboy, there we go.

The dog loped off, with Gary, now weightless again, floating and bouncing above him. They went between some bushes, Gary saying, Whoa, boy, and came out onto a long curving driveway that led to the road, the dog turning his head to give Gary a big grin and a low breathy bark. Gary looked around for something to grab hold of, anything, his toes bumping along the crushed stone driveway, hoping nobody was watching. When they reached the gate the dog made a low ducking turn and headed back up toward the house.

—No way we're going back there, thought Gary, and let go, praying for enough weight to keep him from flying off. He did a slow bouncing roll, covering his head with his arms, and crashed into the hedge, hearing the dog bark appreciatively. Holding onto the hedge, he levered himself upright, judging the power of the effect. There was just enough weight to keep him earthbound, but it could go either way. He picked up a big white stone, one of many that marked the edge of the driveway, and, cradling it carefully against his belly, walked drunkenly out onto the road.

FOURTEEN

Potrzebie

Ten yards down the road a '49 Nash, held together with bailing twine, rattled to a halt alongside him, and the driver, a young kid with a dirty print headscarf and little round green sunglasses, leaned across.

—Okay, he said, loud enough to be heard over the rock music on the radio, Make it good and I'll give you a ride.

Gary squinted at him, shifted his grip on the stone.

—Huh?

—Well, we got those all over. Not painted white, though. Wouldn't it be easier just to paint another one closer to where you're going? Which is?

—Uh, Saint George, I guess.

The kid pushed the door open, giggling. Gary saw a fat joint between his fingers on the steering wheel. He slid into the seat, keeping the rock on his lap. The boy was cackling, his mouth hanging wide open. Gary pulled the door shut and they moved off. The kid took an almighty hit on the joint and offered it to Gary.

—No thanks, he said. I get high anyway.

—You sure do, if you're who I think you are. I think I know who you are, strange visitor from another planet, he croaked, his eyes watering.

—You do, huh, said Gary, hoping Saint George wasn't too far down the road.

The boy cackled. You're the dude fell out the sky, man. Am I right or what?

140

Gary peered at him. And how did you figure that one out?

—Well, Lyn described you, she looked in on you. She's done a story for the *Witness*. And you're outside the Somerville place, I dunno, just a guess, just the vibes. I'm right, huh? Yeah?

Gary sighed, reached for the volume knob and turned the music right down.

—Yeah. That's me. This Lyn? She writes for the paper?

—The *Witness*. My girl. I wish. You're on the front page this week. Some story. Wow. Falling into Ford Somerville's lake, you poor bastard. I'm surprised the guy didn't bore you to death. I'd have crawled back into the water. But you gotta tell me, dude, who the fuck are you, man? What's with the rock?

—This is an Airflyte, right? Gary said, using a standard Kent Treacy sidetracking maneuver. It was the kid's turn to look blank.

—'49 Nash, Gary continued, my old man had one of these. Quite a piece of shit in its day.

—*Airflyte*, the boy laughed, I don't fuckin' believe it, dude. You fell out the sky and now you're in a fuckin' *Airflyte*. Fuckin' A, man, yahahahaha!

They came to a bend in the road and the kid, still helpless with laughter, couldn't get either his head or the Nash around it. They bumped down a rough slope, body panels clanging like backwoods schoolbells, and came to a gently steaming halt just before they hit somebody's farm. There was a nice field with some cows or something in it, and beyond that some trees and the side of a barn with AMPAR painted on it in big yellow letters.

—Oh Jesus, the kid wept, wiping his eyes.

Gary put his head out the window and looked back up the slope. He couldn't see the road from here.

—This will do just fine, he said. Thanks.

The kid shook his head, trying to clear it. Hey, wait up, man . . . no problem.

141

He crashed into reverse and screamed straight back up onto the road, grit pinging off the wheelarches, missing a police car heading back up toward the Somerville place. Gary ducked his head, instinctively but unnecessarily. The kid looked back over his shoulder at the squad car disappearing round the bend, then at Gary.

—You in some kind of trouble?

Gary thought for a minute, while they got back on their way to Saint George. Here was a kid who considered himself an outsider, a rebel.

—Yeah, you could say that. Just don't want to speak to the police, get me?

The kid nodded, eyes narrowed, sucking the last smoke from the roach between his fingertips before flicking it out the window.

—Me neither, man. So why Saint George? Why're you here at all?

—I can't answer all your questions, said Gary, tapping his fingers on the rock in his lap. But I can tell you it has something to do with this rock here.

—Huh?

Gary looked about them shrewdly, and leaned over to whisper in the kid's ear.

—It's *potrzebie*. The real stuff. The Somerville place is thick with it, and he doesn't know it from jack shit. You don't like him too well, huh?

—Aw, he is just a major-league boring dude. And no more a farmer than I am. Still and all, you stole the fucker's rock. He's the kind of asshole that'll come after you for it. Potr . . . what the fuck you say?

—Not a farmer? Told me he's a doctor.

The kid snorted.

—Doctor of bullshitology, perhaps. His old man put him through college. So what's the fucking rock about?

142

Gary sighed. So many questions, kid. You got an inquiring mind.

—I tell you, it's just sooooo boring here. Guy falls out a plane, stealing rocks and shit, that's a trip, man.

—A trip, huh. Is that Saint George?

At the bottom of the hill, a gas station and a convenience store, and some buildings beyond them.

—That's like this side of it. It's a real big town.

—And this is the only road out of it, up to Somerville's place?

—Uh huh.

—You wanna let me out here, kid, I'll be obligated to you. You could do me a major favor, dude.

They reached the bottom of the hill and braked in front of the convenience store.

—Sure. What's that?

—Don't say anything about meeting me until tomorrow, right? Then you can give the story to what's-her-name . . .

—Lyn? Uh, yeah, sure . . . What type rock did you say it was?

—Potrzebie. Listen, you got some kind of bag I can put it in? Looks a mite suspicious, carrying the thing around.

The kid rooted around under the seat, pulled out a drawstring tote bag.

—This okay? It's my sister's.

—Ideal.

Gary was aware that his weight was back to normal, but he wanted to keep the rock with him. He stuffed it into the bag and opened the door.

—Ah, kid, he said, couldn't lend me a couple bucks, could ya?

The kid dug into his pocket, held out a crumpled five-dollar bill. No problem, dude, take it . . . some fuckin' story . . . take care, man . . .

143

Gary pushed the door shut and waved the kid goodbye. As he drove off Gary heard him shout, *Airflyte* yahahahahaha, and turn the radio way up.

—We crashed in your Nash, he sang to himself. Across the road from the convenience store, with a clear view up and down the road, was a diner with a painted sign: Larry's Lunch Pail. The kind of place Ronald McDonald has pretty well put out of business. Gary slung the bag over his shoulder and walked across the empty gas station forecourt, nodding hello to the old guy sitting on an oildrum, crossed the street and went inside. It was empty except for a fat guy in a check shirt and a dirty yellow baseball cap frowning at the newspaper, and a girl behind the counter with a greasy face. He ordered a coffee and a donut and sat at the table in the window. The girl asked him if he was passing through and he said yes, just passing through.

—Saw the Farrell kid drop you off.

—Uh huh, he said, paying more attention to the donut. She let it drop. The fat guy folded his newspaper and held it up for the girl to see.

—See this? Guy fell out a plane right into Elbow Lake and lived to tell the tale.

—Wow, she said blankly.

—Up at the Somerville place. Says here the guy's got exposure, but nothing broken. How 'bout that.

—Wow.

The guy finished his coffee and stood up, wiping his mouth on his hand.

—Well, Diane, honey, I gotta do *some* work today, don't I. My best to Larry.

—Uh huh.

He went outside and crossed the street to the gas station, started talking to the old guy on the oildrum. A few cars went by, heading into town. Gary looked up at the clock on the wall, next to the Joe Montana calendar. One thirty.

144

—I missed the lunchtime rush, huh? he said to the girl, who was just standing staring at nothing.

—Yeah. Uh huh.

Gary dunked the last of the donut and put it in his mouth, realizing he didn't feel too great, like he had a cold coming on or the remains of a bad hangover or something. He went over to where the fat guy had been sitting and picked up the newspaper.

—Okay if I steal this?

—Uh huh.

He took it back to his table. There it was on the front page all right:

MYSTERY MAN IN LAKE PLUNGE

Falls From Plane And Lives To Tell The Tale.

Your Reporter for the *Witness*, Lyn Crowell. Local landowner Ford Somerville got the surprise of his life when pretty daughter Laura (4) spotted a mystery skydiver falling into Elbow Lake. 'Didn't even have a chute,' said Ford yesterday, 'lucky he hit the water.' The mystery visitor from nowhere collapsed before he could tell his story, and Saint George doctor Ken Regis diagnosed exhaustion and exposure, but amazingly no broken bones. The chuteless skydiver, whose identity is unknown, will be able to answer questions after a couple days bedrest in the capable care of Ford's wife Marie. 'We look forward to finding out more about our unexpected house guest,' she says.

Sheriff Roy Gates is also anxious to get some answers. 'At this stage we can't rule out anything,' he says.

145

Saint George has a history of men falling
from the sky; in 1983 Tom 'Bronco' Dibbins
was killed when his parachute failed to open
during that year's Air Meet at Langford Fields.

Gary scanned the rest of the paper without interest. He looked at
the girl at the counter. Someone had unplugged her from the power.
—Okay if I sit here a while? he said. I'm waiting for someone.
—That Farrell kid sure is strange.
Gary opened the newspaper again, making a show of being
interested in it. Then he tore out the article about the mystery
skydiver and put it in his pocket, and sat back and looked out
the window. A little way up the road was a set of lights timed to
stop just about everything coming through, so he'd have plenty
of time to catch Gretchen as she drove by.
About an hour later a police car came down the hill into
town, and he hid guiltily behind the newspaper. Some kids came
in and had sodas and left, talking to each other in a broken,
monosyllabic ur-language Gary didn't understand. A fly landed
on the window and walked up and down it for close on three
hours before Gary swatted it.
Nothing happened at all for a very long time, except the girl
said that the Farrell kid sure was strange. Cars came and went
outside and the old guy on the oildrum over in the gas station
looked as though he might have died. Gary used the time to
drink some more coffee and eat a slice of Larry's homemade
fruit-style pie.
He'd just about got enough strength back to start feeling
impatient when he saw his pickup stop at the lights. He lifted the
bag to his shoulder and left, saying thanks to the girl standing
waxily by the counter with her mouth hanging open. Out in the
street it was early evening, the low sun angling mile-long
shadows. A small kid was hitting his bicycle with a hammer on
the gas station forecourt. Gary saw a black guy sitting next to

146

Gretchen. He waved to them as the lights changed and Gretchen swung the pickup around and braked just by him, jumping down from the cab.

—Oh, Gary, Gary, she said, and put her arms around him, giving him a surprising hug with her face buried in his neck. I have been so worried. I have been so worried.

She let go of him as if suddenly embarrassed, letting her hair cover her face.

Gary broke an awkward silence. Yeah, great to see you, Gretch . . . are we going to stand around saying everything twice? I don't think we have the time. And I've really wrung Saint George dry in terms of excitement.

He climbed into the cab and the black guy slid across to make room for him, Gretchen climbing in after.

—Hi. Gary Wilder.

Lennox shook his hand, felt a little hesitation.

—Wyndham Lennox. I'm from NASA and I have no idea why I'm here.

Gretchen drove up to the lights, which were red again.

—You okay driving? asked Gary.

—If I get us through the town while you talk to Mr Lennox maybe you can take over for a while. If you think it's safe.

Gary looked at her profile. It seemed like weeks. And, yes, she was beautiful. Kind of. He squeezed her arm briefly. She winced, and he noticed the bruise Vandergelder had given her, going yellow.

—Wow, I'm sorry. God, it is good to see you. I really thought I wouldn't. I thought I was never coming back. Jesus, where I've *been*. No camera! Isn't that always the way?

Lennox coughed. I've seen the movie already. But I have to say I'm a little disappointed. Nothing personal, you understand. I'd just rather hoped you'd be flying around.

Gary cocked an eyebrow at him. Take a look in the bag, he said, putting it in his lap. Lennox grunted with the weight.

147

—Okay, what do we have here? It's heavy. It's a rock. And it's painted white. Am I missing something?

—Okay, Mr, er, Lennox . . .

—You can call me just Lennox. Everybody does. It's not demeaning, if that's what's on your mind. I just hate my first name. My wife calls me Wyn, but that's a prerogative of forty years' intimate association. So Lennox will do just fine.

—Okay, sure, Lennox . . . here's the story of that rock.

Gary told them everything he could remember, including the little episode with Vandergelder, as Gretchen drove back through town. It seemed to him as if he were making it up. He felt so normal, and everything had been so impossible. This affected the tone of his voice, which Lennox picked up on, a kind of disbelief, which was what he wanted to hear. In his experience, the more certain people were when recounting the highly unlikely, the less interesting it became. When Gary finished there was silence for a while. Gretchen pulled over to the side of the road. It was getting dark. She rubbed her neck.

—Could you take the wheel for a while? I am totally exhausted. If you start to feel, you know, weird, pull over. I really have to take a nap.

They got down from the cab, Lennox stretching his arms and moving his shoulders around. They stared across an empty parking lot to some low office buildings with copper-colored windows and breathed in the traffic fumes.

—It really is some story, Lennox said through a yawn. Excuse me. It's been a long trip. And I still don't know exactly why I'm here.

—Well, said Gary, as he got behind the wheel, that's the way it happened. Have a little patience. You'll see if your trip was worth it soon enough.

Gretchen leaned against him, her head on his shoulder.

—Hey, he said, I just remembered. He pulled the newspaper

148

clipping from his pocket. You may be interested in this. I'm already front-page news around here. Some proof for you.

They drove off, Gretchen already fast asleep, Lennox peering at the clipping alternately through and over his eyeglasses. Gary reached up and flicked on the cab light.

—So they don't know your name, or where you're from, said Lennox when he'd read it.

—Mystery skydiver, that's me. And an even bigger mystery now I've disappeared.

Lennox looked at Gary, this ordinary-looking guy driving a Japanese pickup with his girl asleep on his shoulder.

—Tell me, he said, what was going through your mind up there? I'd imagine it must have been a pretty intense experience. Pretty mystical, maybe?

Gary pursed his lips, thinking for a while. Mystical? he said at length. No, I don't think so. I don't remember thinking anything. In the sense of coming to any conclusions or anything. There was too much going on. I remember being excited, being kind of relaxed, being cold, real cold, and being shit-scared on the way down. And the voices.

—The voices? said Lennox, thinking, uh oh . . .

—Yeah. Like I was listening to the radio or something. Right up close in my ear.

Lennox didn't like the way things were going here. Disobeying a fundamental law of nature was one thing, he could handle that at a pinch, but voices in the head? The only thing he heard in his head right now was the emergency submerge klaxon.

—Okay, he said reasonably. What were they saying, these, ah, voices?

Gary turned his head and looked at Lennox. You think I'm crazy, right? You do, right? Like you weren't sure before but now you know. These voices, Lennox, not only told me I am the savior of the whole fucking human race but also the final

149

score of next year's Superbowl *and* where Newt Gingrich gets his neckties. Satisfied? Wanna get out?

Lennox grinned, shook his head. I need the ride, he said. I think we take a right up here.

He unfolded a route map on his lap, and Gary listened to his instructions. He couldn't blame the guy if he thought he was crazy.

—Listen, he said, I thought I was going crazy too, when it first happened. I'm still not ruling it out. But don't get hung up on those voices, it was pretty extreme up there, and I reckon they were just, I don't know, audible hallucinations, something like that. They didn't tell me anything.

—So how do you know the whole thing wasn't a hallucination?

—Because Ford Somerville saw me fall into his lake.

—Out of a plane.

—He didn't see a plane. There was no plane. Hell, you talk to the guy, get his story. Nothing stopping you. The beauty of this situation is I don't have to say anything to convince you or anybody what I say is true. You'll find out, you hang around long enough.

—And you're confident it will.

—Yeah, I'm confident it will. And then we'll see where NASA fits in, I guess.

—I don't think there's anything I personally will be able to do to help, if the effect recurs, other than talk to Houston and maybe get you some kind of safe space to do your stuff in, and we can watch. I'm not a physicist, and even if I were I doubt I'd have an answer. If what I hear is true, of course, I can't think big enough to describe the effect it'll have, not just on the scientific community, but on the whole world. But this is crazy. I have to say that I can't help but find it unbelievable at this moment in time. Men can't fly. Newton invented gravity to stop them. I don't see how the effect, as you call it, can be so localized as to happen for just one human being. I mean, why you? Why a human being at all? I don't know. The more I think about this the more I think there's some elaborate set-up going on, with maybe you as an innocent bystander almost. Don't get me wrong. You and Gretchen don't strike me as hucksters. I think you're sincere people and you genuinely believe this is happening to you.

—Oh good, said Gary neutrally.

The miles went by, Lennox helping out at junctions, Gretchen's head on Gary's shoulder. Gary jerked his thumb excitedly at a roadhouse with a neon sign that read 'Jack's', slowing as they drove past.

—Hey hey hey, I know where we are, he said. We used to gig there. The Hi-Tones, my band. Wow. Still called Jack's. Wanna stop by for a beer? Hey, Gretch, wake up, honey, let's stretch our legs a little.

He swung the pickup into the parking lot, empty except for a dented station wagon and a couple of eighteen-wheelers with their cab lights on and drapes pulled.

Gretchen rubbed her eyes. It looks kind of closed, she said drowsily. Where are we?

Lennox showed her on the map.

—Jack's Shack, said Gary. Jesus, we had some good times here. The place burned down once, actually while we were on stage, and they rebuilt it, but they never did ask us back.

—I wonder why, said Gretchen.

There were lights on inside the low black wood building, and the sound of a jukebox as they walked nearer.

—I don't know, Gary, said Gretchen.

—Sure, said Gary. Let's just get some burgers and some beers.

He opened the door and they went inside. There were metal tables with seats bolted to the floor, and a jukebox playing Roger Miller's 'King of the Road'. A guy in a plaid hunter's jacket was sitting on a bar stool, and a big harsh-looking woman stood behind the counter, smoking a cigarette. She had a lot of brittle-looking yellow hair and thick pancake face powder, and was probably bolted to the floor too. The guy drinking at the bar turned and watched as Gary approached, Gretchen and Lennox waiting near the door, looking worried.

—We're closed, said the woman, blowing twin columns of gray smoke down her nose.

—Just a couple beers, he said, then he missed his footing and spun sideways up to the ceiling, popping a fluorescent tube with his knee, sprawled up there for a second, then dropped heavily onto the bar. The silence was broken by a glass rolling slowly onto the floor. Gary felt his shirt get sticky with beer, then he shot back up to the ceiling again and all hell broke loose. The woman was screaming, short repeated deafening screams, her hands to her head. The guy at the bar fell backwards off his stool as Lennox and Gretchen sprinted up. Lennox was standing on the bar pulling on Gary's leg when a fat barechested Hispanic ran through from the back with a sawn-off shotgun wrapped in an oily rag. He waved it at Gary, at Lennox, yelling at the woman to shut the fuck up. Gary dropped into Lennox's arms and they both fell to the floor. Gretchen lunged at the gun barrel as it exploded and blew away a glass shelf of liquor bottles and an Elvis mirror.

Lennox helped Gary to his feet, stepped over the guy on the floor, and said, It's okay, everybody, we're leaving, everyone just calm down here, we're going . . .

He and Gretchen walked Gary to the door, feeling his weight fluctuate wildly, supporting him or holding him down at each step. The woman was still screaming as they kicked open the door and half ran back to the truck, dragging an almost unconscious Gary between them. Dark figures were coming toward them from the parked trucks. They stuffed Gary up into the cab and Lennox got behind the wheel. As they skidded back up onto the highway there was a second shotgun blast and the door mirror exploded, spraying a shower of glass shards into the cab. Lennox floored the gas pedal as headlights flashed and horns sounded everywhere. Gretchen had her arms round Gary's shoulders and his head was lolling. They shot off down a side road.

—Is he okay? said Lennox, brushing splinters of glass from his lap.

—He's white, he looks terrible, his eyes, oh, Gary, Gary . . .

—Put his head down, between his knees . . . watch it now . . .

Gary lurched forward, his head jerked back and he was violently sick into the dash.

—Jesus! shouted Lennox.

Gary groaned, wiped his mouth with his wrist, looked around.

—Larry's fruit pie, he said thickly. Homemade.

FIFTEEN

Everything Happens All At Once

—Okay, Lennox, said Gretchen. Showtime. You ready?

He was sleeping on the couch in his pajamas with a sheet drawn up over his chin. Sunlight was shining through the green and yellow curtains, and she was gently shaking his shoulder.

—Uh?

He took out his earplugs. I'm sorry?

—We're in the kitchen. It's worth the trip.

She picked his glasses up from the floor and held them out to him. He hooked them on and peered at his wristwatch. Just after ten.

—My God, he said, suddenly remembering. What a night. Is he . . . ?

—In the kitchen, Gretchen said, and left him stroking his stubble.

—What the hell have I got into here? he said to himself. He got up, folded the sheet and dressed, getting a clean shirt from his Samsonite Tourister. He didn't like getting dressed before taking a shower, but knew he'd feel uncomfortable walking around a stranger's house in his jammies. He fastened his suitcase and stood it by the end of the couch. Doing little routine things helped him clear his mind.

—Okay, he said, let's see the smoke and the mirrors.

He put his head into the hallway, looked through into the kitchen. He could see Gretchen, barefoot, wearing an extra-large faded blue tee, leaning in the door frame.

—Come on in, Lennox, she said.

No smile, nothing silly about her, no attitude at all. He walked slowly down the hallway. Gretchen was looking up at something. She moved from the doorway to let him in. The blinds were down but the fluorescent ceiling tubes were buzzing. He turned his head slowly to see what she was looking at. Gary was sort of sitting on the ceiling, his back to them, up in the corner of the kitchen, moving around very slightly. He was wearing a teeshirt and a pair of dark blue boxer shorts.

—He's asleep, said Gretchen. Listen.

Lennox listened. Snoring. The guy was snoring. Just bobbing about up there, very gently, perfectly relaxed, one arm across his face, the other floating at his side. Lennox went over to the work surface that ran part way along the wall to get a better view. Gary's arm moved away from his face, his fingers brushing the ceiling. His eyes were closed and Lennox could see his chest move with his breathing. He could also see the guy had a piss hard-on. Lennox shook his head, very slowly.

—Ah . . . none of last night was a dream, was it?

—I think we ought to get him down, said Gretchen matter of factly. Here.

She very gently pulled Gary down, and turned him over, cradling him like a baby.

—Whoa . . . he said suddenly, grabbing Gretchen's arm. What the fuck . . .

—It's okay, you were asleep. You must have floated through.

Gary worked the muscles in his face, sniffed loudly. I came in for a snack, must have blacked out.

He cleared his throat unpleasantly. Excuse me. I gotta use the bathroom. Hi, Lennox.

He lifted his feet to the wall and pushed himself off through the doorway, flying clumsily into the hall and swinging himself around to the left into the bathroom.

155

—One second, said Gretchen. She walked into the hall and shut the bathroom door, came back into the kitchen.

—Simple things, like shutting the door, are a little hard for him.

She went to the sink and filled the kettle. So? she said.

Lennox slowly drew a chair back from the table and sat on it. He looked up at the corner of the ceiling, blinked, and opened his mouth. She plugged the kettle in and leaned back against the sink, smiling at the guy sitting at the table working his jaw up and down and frowning.

—Yes, he said eventually. What we have here is something just too huge and strange to . . . I mean . . . Jesus. Jesus Christ.

He put his head in his hands, pushing his fingers up behind his glasses and rubbing his eyes.

—I have to make some calls, he said decisively, slapping his knees with his hands. How many people have actually seen this thing happen?

—Me, you, Kent, Vandergelder. Some lowlifes in a bar. And half of Utah, for all I know.

—Right. So where are those two right now, Kent and Vandergelder?

—Your guess is as good as mine. You met Kent. He's kind of hard to pin down himself. As Gary pointed out, credibility has never been his strong point. I don't think we need concern ourselves too much with Kent. Vandergelder, though . . . his car's been gone since Gary disappeared, so he's gone with it.

—Why worry? said Gary, floating into the room on his back, holding the top of the door frame. He could see Lennox's amazed reaction and got a buzz from it.

—Where is the guy? she said. Who's he telling about this?

Gary lifted his legs up and stood casually on the ceiling, just for effect.

—Well, I don't think he's telling anyone about it. Not yet, anyway. He's the kind of guy who's always looking for what he

156

can get out of situations. Told me so himself. So what can he get out of this except a reputation as a complete fucking lunatic? Who's he going to tell without coming across like a total propeller head? When he had me on a string he could use me, he was in control. Control's a big thing with the guy, right, Gretch? He's not in control now. And there's the little matter of him kidnapping me and throwing hammers at me and shit. He tells his story, he's thinking about me telling mine. Maybe he thinks I already did, and he's got his alibi fixed. Has he got family near?

—His brother in LA. They never got on. Stanley was the successful one, has his own business. Why?

—Because that's where I reckon he's gone, to have a think about things. Keep his head down for a while. Work out what he's going to do.

Gretchen turned to Lennox. What do you think?

Lennox was staring at Gary, his mouth open. Uh? I'm sorry, I wasn't listening . . . What?

Gretchen and Gary grinned at each other.

—You had some calls to make? asked Gretchen.

—I sure do, said Lennox. But can I first just, ah . . . ? He put a hand out to Gary.

—Sure, said Gary. Go ahead. Find the wires. I'd be grateful.

Lennox held Gary's upper arm and moved him away from the ceiling. There was no resistance. He turned him on his side to float above the table, Gary adopting a ludicrous femme fatale pose, one hand on his hip, the other behind his head.

—Go ahead, he lisped, have your big rough way with me.

Gretchen laughed, slopping coffee down her shirt. Lennox was grinning to split his head. He rolled Gary over, made a hoop of his arms for Gary to pull himself through.

—Okay yet? said Gary. Believe your own eyes?

—This is just the most . . . I better make those calls.

—Phone's somewhere in the front room.

157

—I think, said Gretchen, we'd like to listen to what you have to say, if you don't mind.

Gary put a hand on Lennox's shoulder, letting him pull him through, and Gretchen followed. She found the phone and handed it to Lennox, who sat on the edge of the couch and dialed, keeping an eye on Gary floating gently around the room, doing a little routine for his benefit. Lennox got through to Cy Scott and had one of the more difficult conversations of his career. On one hand, he didn't want to sound like a complete frothing flake, on the other he found it impossible to talk about what he'd seen calmly. Scott kept going on about containment. Containment was key in situations like this. Lennox said there were no situations like this. There was a long pause, Lennox looking serious.

—Okay, he said. It's in my drawer, which is locked. You'll have to bust it open, the key's here with me. Yeah. Also the number here, in the letter, in the tape sleeve. One hour, okay, I'll be here. No, Cy, I swear to God. You should be here. Unbelievable. I had no idea. You can't. Don't even know where to begin. Sure. I'll be waiting. You too.

He put the phone back in the cradle.

—Okay, here's the plan. My super, Cy Scott, he's going to show the Special Projects team your tape, tell them what I've just told him. They'll get back to us right away. There is a Lear jet, so I guess they'll okay that, which just means getting out to LAX.

—This guy, asked Gretchen. How did he sound?

—Same as anyone would. Wary. We've all seen it all at NASA. He watched Gary doing a tuck and a roll. Except this.

—Hey, said Gary, listen up . . .

Someone was knocking on the back door, rattling the handle. Gary eased himself round upright so he could think straight.

—Expecting anyone? said Lennox.

—I'll take a look, said Gretchen. But I think I know who it is.

—Kent, said Gary and Gretchen together.

158

Gretchen went back into the kitchen and peeked through the roller blind over the glazed upper half of the door. It was Kent. She opened the door and he carried something she recognized into the kitchen. Vandergelder's wheelchair, folded up.

—What the hell have you got that for? Where did . . . ?

Then she took in what he was wearing. A retina-wrinkling psychedelic tie-dye shirt over crushed blue velvet bell-bottom pants, strings of colored beads around his neck, and a big button that said 'Say Hi to The High'.

—Is Gary here? Can I get a glass of water?

—They're in the front room. Kent, why have you . . . ?

Kent wheeled the chair through, with Gretchen following, thinking, Patchouli, I can smell thirty-year-old patchouli.

—Yo, Kent, said Gary. Nice duds. I hope Mr motherfucking March of Dimes had his ass in that chair when you folded it up. This is Lennox, from NASA.

—We have met, said Lennox. Excuse me, I think I'll take that shower and a shave.

—Let me find you a towel, said Gretchen.

—Say Hi to The High, said Kent breezily when he and Gary were alone.

—Been home, huh, and your mom never did throw anything out, did she? So what's with the chair?

Kent pulled it open and sat in it, grinning.

—You're going to be very grateful for this fine set of wheels, man. He's gone, it's all empty. I drank his Cuervo. We have to get ready for our meeting, man, it's real important. Everything is under control.

When he said this he held out his hands, giving them the shakes, and made his voice go deep and sinister.

—Shit, said Gary. Yeah, I remember, everything is under controoooool . . . hahahaha!

He did the same thing with his hands. It had been one of those stupid catchphrases the band had used when things were falling

159

over badly but you were too snockered to care. Gretchen came back in. She'd put on a clean check shirt and jeans, and caught her hair up in a ponytail.

—Why don't you get dressed, Gary? We have an event-packed day ahead of us and you don't want to face it in your shorts. At least I don't want to face your shorts.

She shook her head as she heard herself say this. Why was she always telling men what to wear? Gary maneuvered himself out of the room, grumbling something about it being his goddamn house, he'd go butt neckid if he so chose. Gretchen looked at Kent sitting in the chair. So Vandergelder had been too panicked to pack it in the trunk, just hightailed it on out of there. Interesting.

—I would recommend a vocation in music over more traditional careers unreservedly, said Kent, looking at Gretchen with an expression of sage-like sincerity.

—Sure you would, she said fondly, giving his hair a rub.

The front door bell sounded. Gretchen went into the hall and said, Gary, stay in your room a moment, I'll get it. She opened the door, just enough to see it was a cop, and his car parked out on the street.

—Excuse me, miss, he said. Does a Mr Wilder live here?

Gretchen replied without hesitating. No, I'm sorry, he's not at home right now.

It sounded lame. The cop, a young guy with an uncertain expression, flipped open a notebook he took from his breast pocket and glanced at it.

—Are you Gretchen Foster?

—Uh huh. Why?

He flipped the notebook shut and buttoned it back into his pocket.

—There has been an anonymous call from a neighbor about a Perry Vandergelder at 2234? I just checked the place out and would like to ask you a few questions?

Gretchen saw the kids from across the road slouch across the street and come up the drive, leaning against the pickup. They were chewing gum and smoking cigarettes.

—Anonymous call, huh? she said.

—Yes, ma'am. We have to check these things out. There are signs of breaking and entering on the property, and the owner is not on the premises. Could we go inside, please?

—Wait a moment, she said, there are people here. I'll be right back.

She shut the door and the cop turned to look at the kids.

—You live here? he said. No answer, just the sullen tough-guy stares he always got. One of the kids, the one smoking a cigarette, cleared his throat and spat heavily on the driveway. The door opened again.

—Okay, come in, she said, leading him into the living room and pulling back the drapes. Sit down, please. The cop took his hat off and sat on the edge of the couch. He looked around and got his notebook out again.

—So what's this about, this anonymous call? Gretchen said.

—Do you live at 2234 Aspen?

Gretchen sat on the arm of the chair. Until recently.

—Do you know where Vandergelder is at this time?

—No, and I could care less. His car's gone, if that's any help.

—Where did you last see him?

—Christ, said Gretchen, pushing back the strand of hair that fell over her eye, I don't know, at the hospital. His hydro day.

—Can I ask if there was any antagonism between you and Mr Wilder and Mr Vandergelder?

—You can ask. What are we getting into here?

—Could you answer the question?

—I'm not sure I like the way this is going. Is there a charge here? What's this about?

161

—That's what I'm trying to find out. Nobody is being charged with anything.

Gretchen sighed. Vandergelder was pretty pissed when I moved in with Gary here. He's my uncle. Vandergelder, I mean. But there is no antagonism from Gary, it's all from Vandergelder. They don't even speak to each other. Neighbors don't speak to each other round here, they just make anonymous calls to the police.

—And Mr Wilder, do you know where he is at this time?

—He may be at the store, or doing some business, I don't know.

—The store?

—Wilder Sounds. Beach Street.

The cop made some tiny marks in pencil in his notebook. He was here this morning?

—Sure. I guess. He'd left by the time I got up.

—And that's his pickup out there.

—Yeah . . .

The cop made some more little marks, put the notebook away again and stood up, brushing his hat with the palm of his hand.

—Okay, Miss Foster, thank you for your time. If we need to contact you or Mr Wilder we'll be in touch.

Gretchen showed him to the door and let him out.

—Any trouble from those kids? he said, putting his hat on.

—Nothing we can't handle. You might want to talk to *them* about breaking and entering, while you're here.

He gave her a quick glance and walked towards the kids, thumbs hooked in his belt. She shut the door and leaned her head on it, her eyes closed. The phone rang, and she heard Lennox say he'd get it. Then a hand on her shoulder, and Gary's voice.

—You okay?

She turned and looked at him. He was wedged across the hallway, about half-way up, wearing green jeans and a sweatshirt

162

with *Original Bowlings College Style* embroidered over a picture of someone playing golf.

—Look, I put my best shirt on for you. What did the creep want?

Gretchen told him.

—Think he'll be back?

She shrugged.

—Listen, he said, we haven't been able to talk. About the other night.

—What? What about the other night? What other night?

—Jesus, Gretchen, when we, when you . . .

She looked at his eyes. No way was he exactly good-looking. Exactly. She smiled. Kind of fun, wasn't it?

He grinned. Gretchen, I think I, I . . .

She reached out her forefinger and put the tip of it on his lips. Don't say it, right? Things are complicated enough for you right now. Let's see what Lennox is saying.

Gary was grateful for that. He had had no idea what he was going to say, only a vague idea that he should say something.

She took his hand and led him into the front room, towing him over her shoulder. Lennox looked startled and pointed at the windows animatedly.

—The drapes, get the drapes . . .

Gary waited in the doorway while Gretchen shut out the daylight. She saw that the cop and the kids were gone. Lennox was saying, . . . getting urgent, the cops have just paid us a visit. Nope. Absolutely not, but there's a limit to the amount of time we can contain this thing just by pulling the drapes. There's a complication with the neighbor, and my guess is the cops will be back. We need to move on this one. Yeah.

He looked up at Gary and Gretchen, nodding his head and giving them the AOK sign with his thumb and forefinger. He put the phone down and exhaled deeply, his shoulders sagging.

—Okay, we got the Lear arriving at LAX at noon.

—Our own Lear jet, said Gary. Wow.

—Yes, wow. But a little less wow than being able to fly without it, in my opinion. How do you feel?

Gary did a back flip in mid-air, grabbed the back of the chair, and folded himself into the lotus position, rotating slowly over the coffee table.

—Perfectly normal, he said.

—Watch it, said Gretchen, reaching out to stop his head hitting the glass. She turned him right way up and balanced him over the couch.

—Pretty mystical, huh, Lennox? Me, I'm just grateful my shit don't fly.

Lennox raised his eyebrows. Not as grateful as we are, I'm sure.

—Excuse me, you guys, said Gretchen heavily, but we have to get Airboy here out to the plane. Anyone got any suggestions?

—Divert Macy's parade? said Gary.

Kent wheeled himself in on Vandergelder's chair. He needs this more than Vandergelder ever did, he said.

Everyone looked at everyone else.

—Hah! said Gary. Kent got out and helped him in.

—Just need a belt or something, you can wheel me around like a cripple. Wheel me straight up to the plane. Ideal. Is that patchouli? Jesus. I have to make a couple calls, gimme the phone there . . .

Gretchen went out the room to pack some clothes. Kent slumped on the couch with his eyes closed, repeating, Back to earth, down to earth, back to earth, down to earth.

Lennox passed Gary the phone, and nodded his head toward Kent.

—He going to be okay?

—As okay as he ever was, which is okayest by me.

Gretchen threw the belt from a toweling robe into the room, saying, Try this for size. Gary passed it under the seat and

knotted it over his thighs, then dialed the Buena Viva. Luckily
Terry wasn't on the desk. He left a message for Henry that he
was going away on business and wouldn't be able to make the
Monday evenings for a while, but he'd be in touch.

—My old man, he explained to Lennox as he dialed another
number, but I don't think he'll miss me, to be honest. I don't
think he'll even notice. Yeah . . . Carl? Gary. That deal go down
okay with Paul French? Money in the bank? Yeah, I'm back, but
I'm going away again. I'll be in touch. You did? Excellent. One
piece of advice. Never catch anything you can't pass on to
someone else.

He passed the phone back to Lennox.

—Someone else who won't miss me. Kid who worked at the
store just heard he passed an audition for some rock group. Can
you believe this audition stuff? Like it's a job? When we started
you had a guitar, you were *in*. Now, I got to do a few things . . .

Kent stood up. We sure do, he said, and wheeled Gary out of
the room.

Lennox shook his head again, something he was doing a lot of
just recently, and called his wife. Just gave her an idea that he'd
found something pretty important and would be seeing her later.
He hung up as Gretchen set her suitcase down in the door.

—Everything ready? she said.

—I guess so. Where's our cargo?

—I thought they were with you.

Lennox stood up, feeling suddenly stupid and useless, and
Gretchen ran from room to room, calling Gary's name.

—Shit, said Lennox to himself, going into the hall. Gretchen
was staring at a piece of paper tacked to the front door. She
passed it to him.

—I do not believe this, she said, her voice tight with anger.

Lennox took the paper. It said, in curly crayon letters, GONE
TO OBLIVION.

SIXTEEN

Japanese Robot Bomb Factory Socks

—The suits, Kent had whispered in the hall, will put you in a box, man. This had seemed so absolutely correct it struck Gary with the force of a biblical revelation. The suits *would* put him in a box. Simple as that.

—Let's go, he'd hissed, while Kent took a note from his pocket and stuck it on the door. They just went outside and closed the door behind them.

—Take the truck, said Gary, but Kent wheeled him right past it.

—We take the truck, the feds pick us up straight away. We don't need the truck where we're going, man.

Kent pushed him down the curb and across the street.

—Which is? said Gary, his voice lurching as they went up the curb.

—Which is what?

—Where we don't need the pickup for.

—Right. You got it.

—Oh shit, thought Gary, suddenly warming to the idea of a life in a clean room at NASA. They wheeled quickly down Aspen Street in the hot sunlight.

—Okay, Kent, just go by the store, will you? Couple things I need to do if we're going to oblivion.

—Beers would be nice.

—*My* store, Kent, remember?

They went past the house with the busted refrigerator in the yard. An old black guy was sitting out front on a car seat. Gary waved a hand at him.

—Wanna see how many of your kids we can fit in the fridge?

—Motherfucker, said the old guy.

—See? said Gary to Kent. People don't talk to each other anymore.

Kent cut across a vacant lot, the chair leaping crazily over the broken stones and rock-hard gray soil.

—What about your girl, Gar?

Gary gripped the arms of the chair, his teeth shuddering in his head, thinking, Is Gretchen my girl? They got down onto the service road behind the Bargain Hut, weaving between delivery trucks out onto Main Street just opposite Ed's Bait Shoppe, and waited for the lights, looking up at Klub 45.

—I was waiting for the lights in the desert, and now I'm waiting for them on the street, said Kent.

Gary looked up at him wonderingly. The lights changed to Walk and they crossed. Someone shouted, Hey, hippie mother-fucker. Gary raised a finger. They turned onto Beach Street, running over the toes of an old guy selling pencils on the corner. Gary braked by heaving on the grabrims.

—Cool it. The cops.

The blue and white car was stopped right in front of Wilder Sounds. It pulled a U-turn. They hid behind a parked panel truck until it passed.

—They're closing in, man, said Kent. They've got your box ready.

He pushed Gary along the sidewalk, saw something glinting up ahead and bent down to pick it up. It was the hubcap he'd sprung when he scrubbed the curb. He held it out flat, tilting it to catch the sun.

—Woooo, he said. Remind you of anything?

—Yeah. The other three on your car. Spooky, huh?

He handed Kent the keys so he could unlock the shutter. Shit, she's seen us.

Cindy stood in the doorway of the Your Favorite and frowned at them with her head on one side. She shaded her eyes with her order pad and shouted across.

—Hey, Gary? You okay?

—Sure, yelled Gary. Hurt my back.

—The cops were here.

—That's okay.

—Well, you take care now, said Cindy, and went back into the dark of the bar.

Kent lifted him over the step and they went inside. It seemed like years since he'd been here, but there was no mail. Kent stood gazing up at the pegboard while Gary wheeled himself into the office and got the checkbook out of the little cashbox he kept in the desk. He wrote a check, thought about it, ripped it up, wrote another with a much bigger number on it, and sealed it in an envelope, writing *Gretchen – for San Francisco, from Garavity* on it, turning the dot over the *i* into a flower as an afterthought.

Gretchen. Was she his girl? He remembered her with the green plastic pegs in her mouth, waving a pair of Vandergelder's shorts at him. Was she his girl? Part of him wanted to call her right there and ask her, part of him said, Let it go, what happens happens. And that was the bigger part.

He looked around at all the stuff the place had accumulated over more years than he cared to think about, thought about the kids he'd employed, the lean times when he couldn't afford to even do that. The whole store was now, in Carl's words, *like* history. Revisiting your classroom at a high-school reunion, sort of sad but somehow flat and unreal, as if in the absence of your attention things lost their life, folded themselves into fewer dimensions, lost their color. He thought of his dad. The old guy had closed the store years ago, rattled the shutters down and drifted away somewhere, leaving his body behind, colorless, dusty, an empty room.

Gary looked at the Fender Classic calendar, noticing first that

168

it still showed January, second that it was two years old. He looked at the rat's nest of cable hanging from a nail on the wall, the boxes of unidentified bits and pieces all over the floor, thinking, I've been here how many years? How many? From one box to another, that was it. The suits wanted him to spend the rest of his life in a different box, so they could tape electrodes to him and turn him into data. Well, fuck that, and fuck them. Gary Wilder wasn't going to fanny around in a glass room for a bunch of goggle-eyed rocket scientists. He rolled himself back into the shop.

—Kent, you want to reach that jacket down for me? Going to oblivion, gotta be dressed right.

Kent stood on the Marshall cab and unhooked the satin Hi-Tones sport coat from the pegboard.

—Get the Mosrite too, Gary said.

Kent passed down the jacket and carefully unwound the plastic-covered wires holding the guitar to the wall. When he got back down Gary was already wearing the jacket. It was distressingly tight under the arms, and the front was a lot pinker than the back, which had faded over many years' display.

—What do you think?

Kent strummed a slack, out-of-tune chord, winced, and turned the machine heads.

—The sport coat sucked, man, day one.

—Yeah, but kind of neat now, huh?

Kent finished tuning the Mosrite and put the strap over his shoulder. All I *ever* wanted to do, man, was hit a chord so big I could run outside and still hear it playing.

—Keep it. It's a gift. And look after this for me.

He passed him the envelope. Kent looked down at the guitar and Gary thought he was going to cry. The telephone rang.

—We better get out of here.

Kent swiveled the Mosrite over his back and lifted Gary out onto the sidewalk. They locked up and Kent pushed him up the street, toward the desert. They passed the big mysterious Government Building.

—Woh, said Kent. The big mysterious Government Building. Never did find out what those cats were up to.

They hummed a few bars of 'Nerve Gas', Gary stuttering out the words in the chorus. They passed the row of Korean food shops from Mars and the burned-out drycleaner's.

—Why I stopped wearing shoes, said Kent, was I think my Japanese robot bomb factory socks ignited that conflagration.

—You sent your socks to the drycleaner's?

—My mom. I think the fibers combusted. I think they did.

Gary thought it best to let that one drop. The sun was punishingly bright, and he wished he'd got his aviator shades. The sidewalk ran out and Kent pushed him out onto the road, which was just a strip of crushed gray-yellow stone here. They passed the trailer park on the edge of the city limits, and a couple of nasty-looking dogs leaped barking against the cyclone fencing, making it rattle.

—Dogs, said Kent.

They could hear a radio playing, and a guy in zinc sunblock, terrible bermudas and gnarly white legs came out of his Airstream to stare at them.

—Charity cripple march, said Gary. But you gave at the office, huh?

They went past some rusted-up fuel cylinders on the edge of the trailer park and that was it. They were in the desert.

—Uh, Kent, where are we going? I mean, like really?

—Remember K-LUB?

Sure Gary remembered K-LUB. Klub Radio, serving the greater Newdale area in the mid-sixties, set up by the guy that ran Klub 45, and folded along with everything else worthwhile in 'sixty-nine. Transmitter up in the hills about four miles away.

—What about it?

—It's where we're meeting the guy. Off the road up there.

170

Gary rocked his head with frustration.

—Jesus fucking Christ, Kent! What fucking guy for fuck's sake?

Kent stopped pushing the chair and walked around to where he could hunker down and look at Gary at his level. Gary noticed the rubber band had come off his ponytail and his hair hung around his face. Kent adjusted the guitar so it wouldn't hit the ground and made a kind of praying gesture with his big finny hands. If it wasn't exactly the Kent Treacy of twenty-five years ago it was altogether healthier-looking than the nervous geek who'd stopped by the store last week. There was some kind of light in the eyes and they didn't flicker all over the place anymore.

—You should address the problem of your short-term memory loss, Gary, he said, and then he reminded him.

SEVENTEEN

Pencils

Gretchen let the phone ring at Wilder Sounds maybe ten times before letting Lennox make his call, then she went round the house one more time, saying Gary's name, looking in cupboards, stupid places. She went out and tried the garage door, which was locked, and looked in the pickup, squinted up and down the street.

—Shit, she said, and bit her lip. Lennox joined her.

—How hard can they be to spot? A joke hippie from central casting pushing Ollie North in a wheelchair?

They wasted some time tooling up and down the Heights in the truck, getting no response from people they stopped to ask, before heading down into Newdale, where they were stopped at the lights. There was an old guy in a knit cap selling pencils on the corner. He's been there all day, thought Gretchen, and she leaned across Lennox to catch his attention.

—Hey, gimme one of those pencils.

The guy shuffled over. He looked as if he was cold, standing there in the ninety-degree sun.

—Come in a bundle, lady. Two dollars.

—Two dollars? For some pencils? Okay, but tell me, you see a guy pushing another guy in a wheelchair today? One of them a kind of hippie?

The man wiped his nose on the sleeve of his coat. Two dollars the bundle.

Lennox found a couple of bills in his pocket and held them out the window, saying, My treat.

—Well?

The lights had changed and it sounded like a klaxon manufacturers' loudness contest. He took the two dollars, smoothed them out, counted them, folded them up into the palm of his mitten, and gave Lennox the pencils.

—Beach Street, he said, jerking his head over his shoulder. Ran over my goddamn foot. This one. No, it was the other one.

He stared down at his brown nylon zip-up boot.

—Get your attorney onto it! shouted Gretchen, gunning the throttle and swinging the pickup around the turn into Beach Street. They pulled up outside Wilder Sounds.

—Oh ho, said Lennox. Shutters are down, is there another way in?

Gretchen looked above the single-story row of stores to the high blank side wall of the cinema on Main Street.

—I don't think so. It backs up against the movie house there.

—Then they ain't here.

She turned the ignition off and got out onto the sidewalk, looking around.

—I'm going to check out that bar over there. Coming?

Lennox got out and they crossed the street and went into the Your Favorite. There were some men with their suit jackets hung over chair backs eating a business lunch in one of the booths, and a couple of drinkers at the bar watching television, one of whom turned to look Gretchen up and down before turning back to the game. There was a blond girl behind the bar in a little red dress with a gingham apron and *Your Favorite* embroidered over the left breast.

—Hi there, said Cindy. What can I get you folks?

—Actually, I was wondering if you could help us?

173

—And how could I do that, honey?

The drinkers at the bar hooted derisively as someone fumbled a play.

—We're looking for the guy who runs the store over there, Gary Wilder?

Cindy leaned forward on the bar and looked at Lennox. Are you the feds?

Lennox smiled and shook his head. No, ma'am.

—We're friends. We expected to find him at the store. You know Gary?

—Sure I know Gary. He was by earlier. Is he okay? He was in a wheelchair, being pushed by a hippie. Just after the cops had a look at the place. Weird.

—Did you see where he went? asked Lennox. Which direction he took?

Cindy shook her head. One of the guys at the bar snapped his fingers for another beer.

—Sorry. Excuse me.

Gretchen said thanks and they went back out onto the street.

—Well, said Lennox, one hand on his hip, the other scratching his head, we're damned close, wherever he is.

They looked both ways along Beach Street, the traffic along Main to their left, the town and the road sort of fading out to their right.

—Out of town doesn't look too promising, he said. That road go anywhere?

—No, said Gretchen, which is why I think they went that way. Kent said something about losing his car in the desert. Maybe they've gone to find it. The note said gone to oblivion, remember. That doesn't sound like downtown Newdale to me. But I could be wrong.

Lennox smiled at her. Sharp. I'm impressed.

—Too easily.

—I don't think so. I'm too old. You're okay, Gretchen.

174

She snorted, and they got back in the pickup and headed out of town.

—I mean it, said Lennox. You're okay.

—You know absolutely nothing about me.

—What's there to know?

Gretchen gave him her lopsided smile. Oh, you'd be surprised.

—So surprise me.

She inhaled, held her breath a moment, as if making up her mind whether to tell him something.

—Well, she said, I robbed a bank once. Me and this guy. Okay people don't rob banks, right?

—Wow, said Lennox, shaking his head in wonder. No kidding. He looked at her, thinking, Yeah, I can see it, got hooked up with some punk.

—Well, Gary left us his rock, anyway, he said, and hefted the drawstring bag up on the seat.

—Crazy guy, said Gretchen, scanning both sides of the street. What do you think about him now you've seen him do his stuff?

Lennox turned his head to look at the burned-out drycleaner's.

—I can't quite get a handle on the guy, and I'm pretty good at reading character.

—You reckon, said Gretchen, giving him a look.

They passed the trailer park.

—Hold it, said Lennox, seeing the old guy in warpaint staring at them from the step of his Airstream. Gretchen braked and Lennox waved to him.

—Excuse me? Have you seen someone in a wheelchair come by?

—Charity cripple thing, he said. Crock of shit, you ask me.

A big mad-faced dog flew past him, nearly knocking him off the step, and launched itself at the wire fence, hanging from it about four feet from the ground.

—Okay, sir, thank you, said Lennox. Let's get out of here.

Ahead of them just parched scabs of coarse grass and chalky

175

soil stretching up on either side to the mountains on the distant horizon.

—What's that? said Gretchen, pointing up ahead.

The brightness was making Lennox's head hurt. He could just make out a dark dot way in the distance, off to the left. The track was getting bumpier and he had to use the grabhandle above the door to keep from getting thrown about. Little by little the dot got bigger, and there was a quick glint of something bright on it.

—It's a car, said Gretchen. Kent's?

It took maybe another ten minutes to reach it, the truck lurching all over the place, Gretchen struggling to keep it on line. When they stopped and turned the engine off the silence wrapped them like a blanket, and the desert suddenly became the biggest place in the world.

—Don't say it, Lennox. They ain't here either. God-damn them.

They stepped down into the shadeless heat and looked around them. The silence began to get scary.

—Let's take a look in here, said Lennox, and pulled open the driver's door of the battered little car.

—Yowch, shit, Jesus! he yelped, waving his hand and blowing on it. That metal's red hot.

They left the doors open for a while until they could bear the heat inside. Gretchen creased her face up.

—Yeeuch, what a mess, really . . .

She sifted through the garbage on the floor.

—Here's the registration, said Lennox, pulling it from the glovebox. Registered to a Kent Treacy. That's our boy. Whole bunch of stuff in here, have a look at this . . .

He passed Gretchen a fistful of paper. She leafed through it, flyers, mostly, a couple of letters concerning the funeral of Edward Taylor Treacy, and a letterhead which caught her eye immediately.

176

—Paydirt, she said, dropping everything else on the floor.

Lennox leaned over and she smoothed the sheet out on her lap. At the top were the words Oblivion Records, in swirly pink and green letters.

—*Dear Kent*, she read. *Thank you for your call*, blah blah, blah blah, *reunion album*, blah . . . here we are . . . *be pleased to meet you out at the old K-LUB transmitter at the end of Beach Street.* And there's directions. We passed it. I'm relieved, I have to say it. You know, oblivion and all that stuff. He's just gone to see a guy about a recording contract.

They walked back to the pickup, Lennox frowning.

—But why? Why now? Why did Gary go with him? Doesn't make sense.

Gretchen laughed, and gave him a punch on the upper arm.

—*Now* you're getting it!

EIGHTEEN

Styrofoam

Tony DiSanto put his feet up on the desk and looked at his watch.

—Wanna give 'em another hour?

Alex Colcannon was standing at the window, finger hooked in the twisted venetian blinds, peering out at the desert. Radio K-LUB was a sand-blasted concrete bunker with a narrow horizontal strip of densely scratched glass and an antenna coming out dead center from the flat roof. Over the years grit and dust had blown in a drift right up one side over the roof, blending the block into the hillside. Parked out front next to the blockhouse holding the long-dead generator was DiSanto's 4x4. Inside the studio everything had been stripped out long ago except for the big custom-built desk, now with gaping holes where the electronics used to be, and a couple of busted-up chairs.

—I have all day for this, said Alex quietly. You work with Kent Treacy, you become acclimatized to his methods. Necessarily. Or you don't work with him. It may be worth it.

Alex Colcannon was tall, slim, with carefully managed receding sandy hair, and wore a white oxford shirt, buttoned at the neck, khakis, and a pre-war Reverso. He'd flown from New York to take a look at some promising warehouse space off the Strip that he was considering opening as a West Coast gallery space. He'd received various letters from Tony over the years, trying to get The High back together, and was using this trip as an opportunity to maybe take the idea a little further. That depended on how well Gary and Kent came over. He relished the element of surprise today. See how they reacted to his turning up out of the blue like that.

—Another beer, Al?

Alex raised an eyebrow. *Nobody* called him Al.

—No, thank you, he said, without turning from the window.

Tony took another Coors from the big styrofoam cooler.

—I think, said Alex, we have visitors.

Tony joined him at the window, peered through the thick, shot-blasted glass. Up over the ridge came something weird. Cripple in a wheelchair being pushed by a hippie with a guitar slung across his back. Tony went to the open door for a clearer look.

—Yeah, he said, that's Kent. The guy in the wheelchair, I dunno . . . any ideas?

Alex looked past Tony's shoulder, keeping back in the dark.

—My God, it's Gary. Gary Wilder. He's an old man, look at him.

Gary had been reassured by Kent's definition of oblivion. There'd been a moment back there when he'd entertained a kind of staring-into-the-sun geronimo fatalism, feeling he was sitting next to James Dean on his last ride, but then he realized he'd always hated James Dean with his stupid mumbling and pathetic fucking eyebrows, so right now signing a recording contract made as much sense as anything else. Which, as he had to admit, was no sense at all. They could see the antenna about a quarter-mile before they made it to the station.

Gary turned his head to look at Kent and said, Remember driving up here when 'Surferama' came out, trying to persuade that jock to flip it?

Kent stopped for a minute, wiping his palms on his thighs. It was only the weight of the chair he was pushing, but it was still tiring in the heat.

—Like it was yesterday, or even tomorrow. Time's weird, man.

He pushed the chair up over a crest in the track. Here we are, man, he said. End of the line.

They were looking at the silted-up bunker of the radio station and the mess of stanchions and rusted guyropes tangled up around the base of the antenna. Someone in a blue shirt was standing in the open door, waving at them.

—That's Captain Oblivion, Kent said, and pushed the chair up to the building.

Tony DiSanto came down the steps. Kent, how you doing? Gary? Tony DiSanto. Hey, you brought your guitar. Great. But, Gary, forgive me, I wasn't expecting . . . I mean, Kent here never told me . . .

Gary waved his hand dismissively. Damaged my back. Temporary thing. Up and about in no time.

Kent refused Tony's offer of help and lifted Gary up the steps into the relative cool of the empty office. Tony looking surprised, thinking, The skinny guy's stronger than he looks.

—Got kind of a surprise for you in here, said Tony, opening the door into the studio, letting them go through first.

Alex turned slowly from the window, his arms folded, expression coolly quizzical.

—We meet again, he said, arching an eyebrow.

Kent went straight to the cooler. Got any Corona?

Gary slapped the arms of his chair and cackled coarsely.

—Hahahaha, Alex Colcannon, you bald fuck!

Alex frowned. This was not going as expected.

—Time has wrought changes on us all, Gary. I'm sorry to see you, ah, as you are, so early in life.

—I tell you, Gary said, catching the Coors Kent threw him, life is full of surprises. Don't you worry about me. What brings you out west? Just to give us your profile?

Alex looked at Tony for help, his face strained.

Tony flopped into the chair behind the desk, sending up a little cloud of dust.

—I've been in contact with Alex over some years, he said. Luckily he was able to include this meeting into his heavy art business schedule, for which we're all obligated, and also for your own presence here. This is really an exciting moment in the history of the medium of rock and roll.

Gary spun the chair round so he could twist his face up at Tony. It is?

Tony gestured meaninglessly with his hands and laughed politely.

—Alex and I have great hopes for the successful exploitation of The High's reunion. It's something we all can benefit from, and the whole area of rock and roll music in general. Alex's idea . . .

—Whoa, said Gary, holding his hands up. You mean this is *his* idea? Kent, you want to say something?

—Styrofoam, said Kent, peering into the cooler.

There was a puzzled silence.

—Okay, said Gary, let's hear the great man's idea.

—Your attitude is tiring, Gary. I'd forgotten just how tiring. No-one's forcing you to be here.

—Gentlemen, said Tony, clearing his throat, let's all just back off a way so we can get this thing we have here into some kind of perspective. Okay? Right. We're all busy guys. No-one's suggesting The High re-form indefinitely, with all the commitment that would entail. What we're looking at here is a mutually advantageous, short-term arrangement that would benefit us all, and, as I've said, the whole rock and roll context itself . . .

Gary didn't pay too much attention to the rest. He was mad at Alex for talking to this Italian behind his back about something that affected him. The High had been his band. So had The Hi-Tones, and so had Gary Wilder and The Wild Ones, and Alex hadn't even been in that band. Gary had brought the guy into

181

the group, given him his break, and now the ungrateful son of a bitch was organizing reunions all over the place and telling Gary he didn't have to be involved. Well, fuck him as well as the rocket scientists. And there was also the matter of his weight. The belt was beginning to bite into his thighs. He could feel blood going to his head, making it throb. And when he stopped gripping the arms of the chair and relaxed, which was an effort because of how mad Alex was making him, his arms very definitely fell up. He could feel some kind of gravity affecting him, but it was all skewed. It wasn't the invigorating buzz of weightlessness this time around, there was something more, as if he was getting his weight back but in the wrong direction.

—Well, well, well, said Alex dryly, interrupting Tony's flow. Who have we here?

Between the buckled venetian blinds they watched a dirty black pickup bounce up into view and brake in a cloud of dust. Gary had recognized the signature sound of his own badly maintained cylinder block. He nudged Kent's foot with his own.

—You okay?

Kent looked up at him.

—Styrofoam, man. The whole deal is styrofoam.

Gary knew exactly what he meant. Tony went out of the studio and he heard him talking to Gretchen. He felt the chair shift under him and held tight onto the steel rims. The chair was beginning to creak. Alex was looking at him curiously, noticing his face getting redder, and sensed something odd, something he couldn't pin down.

—Are you unwell, Gary?

Before he could answer, Gretchen and Lennox came in.

—Gary? she said, and Gary heard the strain in her voice. Who are these people? I mean, what are you doing here with these people? They have nothing to do with us, I mean nothing . . .

Tony came forward, holding his hand out. Tony DiSanto, DiSanto Promotions. Alex Colcannon.

Gretchen looked down at his hand in disbelief.

—Excuse me? Who gives a fuck? I mean, who honestly gives a fuck? Gary, let's get out of here.

Gary looked around at the variety of facial expressions Gretchen had lit up. I need a minute with Gretchen here, he said.

She pushed Gary back into the lobby, giving Lennox a quick grimace of frustration. Gretchen shut the door behind them, just catching Kent's heel as he threw a rock and roll shape with the guitar. She knelt on the dusty floor in front of Gary. Her voice was quieter but the stress was still evident.

—What's happening, Gary? Just tell me. All these new guys all of a sudden. Who needs them? They've got nothing to do with anything. This is about *us*, isn't it, Gary? Let's just go, just get back to the plan. Remember the plan?

—The thing about situations like this is that there are no situations like this, he said heavily. Lennox got it right.

He struggled out from under the belt and dropped straight up to the ceiling, landing on all fours with a grunt before getting to his feet.

—This is what's happening. I don't have to tell you. Fuck it. Look at me. I've got my weight back but it's the wrong fucking direction. Everything's turned upside down. You're right. Those guys in there are nothing to do with it. They're just part of Kent's fucked-up approach to life. Which does have its own integrity, incidentally. But I have to ask what does *anything* have to do with me anymore? I don't know about Lennox either. I'm the guy walking on the fucking ceiling round here and it does give me a kind of unique perspective. I mean, shit, Gretchen, we can't just get *married* now, and live happily ever after, not even in Los Angeles . . .

He walked around the ceiling to prove his point, kicking the bulbless lamp like a dead flower head, and stood looking out of the door. He could see the pickup and Tony's 4x4 hanging off

183

the dusty ground above his head, and the cloudless blue sky below his feet, just across the threshold.

The word *married* was still resonating for Gretchen, and she was having trouble dealing with it. She felt herself getting closer to Gary as he was getting further away, in spite of herself, and she wasn't happy with it. Suddenly everything seemed pointless, lost, over, and she'd been hurt all over again, and for nothing. For nothing.

—Gary, we have to get you to NASA, she said, hearing the hopelessness in her own voice. There's nowhere else to go. You can't control this, it's out of control . . .

He turned from the doorway and bent his head around to see her face better. She looked tired and very sad, but Gary could still see her as she'd been as a little girl. Vulnerable.

—Why'd you run out on us? she said, a little anger showing.

He sat down on the ceiling with his back to the door.

—Just something that Kent said. They're going to put me in a box. They're not going to let me go, Gretchen. What he said was true.

Gretchen stood up and reached out to hold his hand. What are you going to do, Gary?

—I've never known the answer to that. Today's no different. And you know what? First time for a week that I feel normal. No buzzing in the bloodstream, no queasy floating sensations, I feel completely . . . usual? To me, right now, it's the rest of the world that's upside down, that's all. All the times before, when I felt it was over, I knew I was kidding myself. This time, I know it's true. It's over, no going back, overturned, head over heels . . .

—Like being in love, she said, half to herself.

The door opened and Alex appeared, instantly dumbfounded, frozen to the spot, his face a stupid gaping mask.

—Oh shit, said Gary, stumbling back.

Alex found his voice.

184

—What kind of stunt is this? What's . . . ?

He watched as Gary moved away from him, realized it was both completely natural and yet simultaneously against nature, unthinkable, horrible. He couldn't cope with it, became suddenly angry.

—You *stupid* . . .

The others were there now, and the lobby was crowded. Alex was shouting. Lennox put his hand on his shoulder, tried to calm him down. Tony DiSanto was laughing, but there wasn't anything funny about it. Alex stabbed a finger at Gary. He's a fucking freakshow. *Look* at the guy. Jesus, I'm out of here.

He charged at Gary, pushing him in the chest, knocking him over. Gary tripped back over the wall above the door and fell out. Just fell out, was gone. There was a moment of silence and then Gretchen screamed, ran outside. Lennox elbowed Alex out of the way and followed her, leaping down the steps. She was walking backward away from the building, pointing up.

—He's there! she shouted.

Lennox looked up and saw Gary clinging to one of the stanchions supporting the antenna, about thirty feet up. His legs were swinging above him and he was struggling to keep his grip. Gretchen was scrabbling up the dune at the side of the building.

—Just what the fuck is going on here? said Tony shrilly, joining Lennox. They stared at Gretchen, now on the roof, and Gary, sliding up the angled stanchion toward the central antenna.

—I was going to ask you that, said Lennox.

Gretchen squeezed inside the cylindrical cage surrounding the service ladder and climbed until she was the same height as Gary, about ten feet away from him. He'd hooked his arms over the metal rod and was trying to pull himself back down.

—Slide up, Gary! she shouted. I can't reach you here. Go up.

—I'm trying to, fuck it, he grunted.

Gretchen shook the cage in frustration. Down, I mean. Let yourself down. I'll climb up to where I can reach you. Don't let

185

go, just let yourself slip . . . yeah . . . that's it . . . I'm coming,
I'm with you . . .

On the ground Alex was insisting Tony drive him away from
there. He was stabbing the buttons on his portable phone.

—I want *no* part of this. *Answer* me. Tony, the keys, God *damn*
it . . .

—Got a rope? said Lennox.

—In the truck. I'll get it, said Tony.

Lennox started to climb the slope to the roof. He could hear
Gretchen and Gary shouting to each other but couldn't make out
the words. Kent overtook him up the slope, playing silent chords
on the guitar. Gretchen saw them all about thirty feet below her,
the dark-haired guy running from the truck with a rope.

—Hang in there, Gary! she yelled, They're getting a rope,
we'll get you.

She was at the top of the ladder. There was no more up for
her to go. A corroded box of smashed-up electronics was just
above her head, the antenna rising behind it, as thick as her thigh
at that point. Gary was sliding up toward her, getting nearer.
She heard a yell from below, and looked down to see Lennox
waving the rope.

—They're coming, Gary, just a little further . . .

She reached out from the cage, her fingertips just brushing his
jacket. She grabbed the hem, just as his sweaty, aching fingers
lost their grip. Gretchen, crushed hard up against the steel box,
felt the satin rip away. Somehow he caught her wrist. She felt his
wet, weak grip slip off over her hand, Gary yelling, God oh
God. He clung to the antenna, wrapping his legs around it. His
jacket hung in shreds up from his shoulders, pink flags against the
blue of the sky.

—Gretchen, God, I can't hold it anymore.

His hands ceased to grip, slipped, squeaked. He felt the hot
metal slide up over his face, heard Lennox shout something just
above him, and then Gretchen's voice, but he was falling down

the tapering steel like a fireman on a pole. Looking up, he saw Gretchen leaning out, throwing the end of the rope. The first time it hit his back, but the second she couldn't make it reach him. He saw the roof of the radio station, and a small figure dancing in bright colors. He'd reached the tip of the mast, and his legs swung down into nothing. He felt the whole blue round earth tug on the antenna, and thought he saw Gretchen's face, one last time.

—It wants to fly . . . Gretchen . . .

And he let go.

Down on the ground, Kent touched Gretchen's shaking shoulder. It's okay, he said softly. It's okay. He's gone to cut the grass.

And he struck a chord so big even Gary heard it.

Gary Wilder – Discography

GARY WILDER AND THE WILD ONES

Surferama/Big Shot	Regality RG 756–9	1962
Snow Shoes/Hava Nagila	Regality RG 737B	1962?

THE HI-TONES

Surferama/Nerve Gas	Regality RG 876–00	1964
Nerve Gas /Picture Garden	Kosmos Z-66	1965
Shady Tree Party/Blisterfinger	Tri-Berry 40001	1966

Bikini Au-Go-Go OST (LP)
Shady Tree Party/Angie's Summer/Bikini Au-Go-Go

	Radiant Pictures RLP1	1966

THE HIGH

Lilac Lace/People Pretty People	Power Of Plants POP 22	1967
Citadel Of Your Face/Nerve Gas	Which's Brew 34–812	1967
Mind Bicycle/Little Peach Persuader	Trezure Chest CHEST 7	1968

Notes: All three recordings of 'Nerve Gas' are different takes.
All the above material except RG 737B has been collected and reissued on the
Saycadelik CD 'Say Hi To The High' (SAYCD 54).
CHEST 7 may only feature Gary Wilder plus session musicians.

Without Gary Wilder:

The High   Back To Earth (CD)   Oblivion OBVN 1–94–03   1994
With Kent Treacy and Alex Colcannon
plus the drummer and rhythm guitarist from the Sand Pythons.
Ten tracks, including another reworking of 'Nerve Gas', a thirty-minute
instrumental 'Cutting Grass', and 'When Gary Gets Back' with vocal by Gretchen
Foster.

Related interest:

Biggest Hits From Magical Mexico
                               Wondergold TSN299   197-?
(instrumental album featuring an uncredited Kent Treacy on guitar)
The Snotz   Zip Up Punk/Your Germs
                               Kill Kill Kill KKK-3   1976
(New York band featuring Alex Colcannon on bass)
Death Spasm   Bloodsperm Bitches Ampar AMPCD 12   1994
Gretchen Foster
               When Gary Gets Back/San Francisco Days
                          Legacy 6359   1995